Frank Moorhouse was b
Nowra. He has worked as an editor of small-town newspapers and as an administrator, but in the seventies became a full-time writer.

He has won a number of literary prizes including the Australian Literature Society's Gold Medal for 1989. *Forty-Seventeen* was given a laudatory full-page review by Angela Carter in the *New York Times* and was named Book of the Year in 1988 by the *Age* newspaper in Melbourne, and 'moral winner' of the Booker prize by the London magazine *Blitz*.

For a time, Frank Moorhouse lived in France where he wrote the highly praised *Grand Days*, the first volume in his Palais des Nations novel series set at the League of Nations in Geneva between the wars, and the essays for the Sydney and Adelaide *Reviews* that became *Loose Living*.

OTHER BOOKS BY FRANK MOORHOUSE IN PICADOR:

The Americans, Baby
The Electrical Experience
Lateshows
Forty-Seventeen
Grand Days
Loose Living

7–
mB

Futility & Other Animals

frank MOORHOUSE

Pan Macmillan Australia

First published 1969 by Gareth Powell and Associates.
Published 1973 by Angus & Robertson Publishers.

This Picador edition
first published 1996 by Pan Macmillan Australia Pty Limited
St Martins Tower, 31 Market Street, Sydney

National Library of Australia
cataloguing-in-publication data:

Moorhouse, Frank, 1938– .
Futility and other animals.

ISBN 0 330 35688 7 (pbk.).

I. Title.

A823.3

Printed in Australia by McPherson's Printing Group

For W. S. and J and T who meant so much to me.

The central dilemma is that of giving birth,
of creating new life.

Contents

Confusion

The Story of the Knife 1
What Can You Say? 15
"No Birds Were Flying Overhead, There Were No Birds to Fly" 21
Anderson, How Can There Be a Baby and No Crying? 29
Across the Plains, Over the Mountains, and Down to the Sea 39
Rambling Boy 42
The First Story of Nature 47

Sickness

Nish's Sour Desire 59
Nish 61
Dry Munching 64
Bread, Sugar, and Milk 67
I Am a Very Clean Person 70
Will Power + Natural Sex-Drive + Intelligence + Personal Organisation + Aggression = Sexual Success 76
Lou Shouted "Hey!" 82

Bravery

Walking Out 91
I Saw a Child for the Three of Us 99
Ten Years 102
The Train Will Shortly Arrive 107
Apples and Babies 125
Anderson's Story 134
Dead 141
Futility and Other Animals 145
The Second Story of Nature 150
The Third Story of Nature 164

CONFUSION

The Story of the Knife

"THE KNIFE was in the duffle coat—with the methedrine and *Herzog*."

"Shit."

"Someone might have taken it by mistake. They might return it."

"Oh yes."

"I'm sorry."

"It's not your fault." She stood before him, contrite, perhaps a little frightened. Her youth showed when she faced him defensively.

"All things pass," he said. "That's folk fatalism. Perhaps the time of the knife is over." The time of the knife. She did that to him. Twenty-year-olds were always saying things like that. The knife was stolen. There was nothing portentous about that. In fact the duffle coat was stolen—the knife just happened to be in it.

She had moved over to the refrigerator and taken out a flagon of dry white and was pouring a glass.

"You want some?"

"No, I'll have a scotch—with two ice cubes."

"I'm sorry."

"I'm not blaming you. It doesn't matter."

She went about getting him the scotch, running water on the ice tray to free the ice.

Then without previous hint, quite unpredictably, she said: "Roger, I think our time together is finished. I think it's time I moved out."

Well.

He first thought to argue against it and hold her. Then he let go to a feeling of resignation which was stronger. She was probably right. It probably was finished. If she *felt* it was over then perhaps ipso facto it was. It wouldn't shatter him. But weren't twenty-year-olds too much. They always *knew* and they acted so biblically as though life was a series of mystically revealed events. A time for every purpose. They woke on a morning and were able to feel and believe that from *that* day "things would be different" or something. Anne, he thought, Anne, when you're twenty-eight you'll be sure of different things. You'll be sure that life is confusing, you'll be sure that you can't be certain, and you'll know that life doesn't change but goes on in eccentrically undulating cycles. He caught sight of his thinking and was embarrassed by it.

She put the scotch in front of him.

"If that's the way you feel, Anne."

She sat opposite him on the other side of the table.

"I've been ignoring signs, Roger. I think our feelings have changed. It's almost as if the knife marked something—symbolically. It was a symbolic thing."

Twenty-year-olds were *too much.*

His indifference left him without a reply. Now that they were living in the city their affair was certainly flatter. But pleasant. At the cabin where there had been fantasies, it had been a digression from their mainstream, a suspension from routine, and other things.

It was cold living in the cabin above the gorge. Perry had left a portagas stove but the gas had all but gone and they were conserving it.

"I could light a fire in the middle of the room. Underneath the matting it's cement."

"You'll smoke us out," she said. She was painting, an army blanket around her shoulders. She had on his navy blue polo neck jumper he used for sailing. Her knees were drawn up to form an easel.

He drank from his glass of claret. He dipped his finger in the claret and wrote her name on the table. He dipped his finger again and sucked it. He liked sucking. Sucking nipples. Sucking her fingers. Sucking cocks? No, not that. He couldn't come at that.

"I'm going to buy a knife tomorrow," he announced.

"Great."

Her sweet typical reaction. Why did she think it was "great"—as though she was expecting him to buy a knife?

"Do you really think it's 'great'?"

"Yes, I want you to have a knife."

He smiled. Oh, the sweetness of it. He moved over to her and kissed her hair. He knelt and hugged her hunched knees.

"It's a man's-thing," she said, her hand on his face. "You're my man—down here anyway. I just want you to have a knife."

"I'm not buying a sheath knife."

"You'll know what sort of knife to buy."

He rested his head on her feet. Times such as these, when she spoke with female authority, when she acted with such sure emotional touch—these times made him swell as a man. Her touchings, her words, her movements, the way she handled food, the way she cut an onion, the way she painted, and the way she washed herself.

Was he playing with manhood or something? Or was she playing with womanhood? Or was it just a part of the thing they had going between them? How could she know, at her age, what she did to him? She'd had a kid but that was a mistake and it did not make her a woman. She was just twenty. She was playing it by ear and it was all so right. But perhaps it was his private fetish. Should you tell the other person that they were catering for a fetish? Was a secret pleasure dishonest? But Christ, feeling this way wasn't a fetish. This was the way he should feel. Like man, it's the real thing. It's the real bit, man. Like you wouldn't want to know.

Next day they walked the four miles to the store along the track to where it met the bourgeois asphalt of the town.

He told the girl in the shop that he wanted a knife with one long blade, a short blade, a can opener, a needle, a pair of tweezers, a screw driver, and a bone handle.

She handed him one to look at.

"No—I'd like to look at that one," he said, pointing to a black bone-handled knife. She handed it to him. He opened up its implements—fanned out like a sun god. He half knew then that this was the one. Anne stood silently while he compared it.

The black bone-handled one had everything except the screwdriver. But it was the one.

"I'll take it," he said to the shop girl.

Anne came up against him. "It's a splendid knife," she said, and ran her finger along its body. She picked it up and held it against her face before the assistant wrapped it. "It's a knife for all seasons—a knife for the backwoods."

The shop girl looked at her.

"I'll skin animals," he said, "and defend you and cut ropes and carve wood."

The shop girl looked away.

Outside he unwrapped the knife. "It's a good knife."

"Yes, yes, yes," she said, putting her head against him as they walked away from the town, off the bourgeois asphalt and along the track which became wilder and then tenuously reached the cabin.

He made a strap for the knife. He found a leather strap hanging from an army water bottle in the shed behind the cabin. He cut a length from it which included a buckle at one end. The leather had dried but he rubbed it with oil. On one side it was finished and on the other rough. The oil he rubbed into it gave it back some suppleness. He tapered the free end and bevelled the edges. He used steel wool to clean the rust from the buckle until it was a dull, smooth metal gleam. He oiled the buckle. Giving the strap another application of oil he hung it in the shed until the afternoon.

In the afternoon the leather was alive. It had regained its

full suppleness and a sheen. He slapped it on his thigh. Threading the strap through the lanyard loop of the knife he then buckled the strap through his belt. It hung about eight inches.

He went into the cabin.

"Look."

"Oh fine—it looks so fine."

She came over to him and handled the knife.

"When I'm down here I'll wear it out like this. In the city, I'll put it in my pocket."

"Yes, wear it all the time—in the city too—it should go with you everywhere."

Next day he carved her name in a tree.

"It doesn't hurt the tree does it?" she asked.

"A tree doesn't mind being cut with a real knife for a real reason."

He first cut away the bark to reach the wood of the bole —thigh white.

He carved: "Roger and Anne loved in this place". He felt that the phrasing "loved in this place" carried the correct interpretation of their affair—more a passionate affection limited in time than a deep important love. He hoped Anne understood it that way.

One day they went to the shoreline and with the sea swirling around their legs they prised oysters on the sea-pocket rocks, snatching them between the onrush and retreat of the sea, eating them from the knife blade. The knife hung from its strap around his wrist, the leather strap dark wet from the sea.

"God", he said, wiping his face with a dripping hand, "oysters—the sea—and you."

"And the knife," she said smiling. They kissed with the knife caught between them, hard against their chests and the sea surging around their knees, cold and uniting.

They drank wine that night with some methedrine until they both burned brightly.

"You don't talk about everlasting love," she said, "and that's what I like about the way we are."

"Don't you believe in everlasting love?" he asked. He was always intrigued by the way she catalogued herself.

"No I don't—do you?"

"I don't know, Anne—I think probably some people can have everlasting love."

"Really passionate everlasting love?"

"Everlasting in the sense that it is sexually and in every other way alive—and goes on for years."

"How many people do you know who have it," she asked disbelievingly.

"Perhaps one or two couples—that's among my friends—but then, my friends are not prone to everlasting love. Not that they don't try."

He saw some who had tried and failed—Sean, Robyn, and Jimmy and Jeanette, Anderson and Sally and saw them in frozen stances of pain or anger or disillusion.

"Love lasts for as long as it's there— and it's too fragile and vulnerable to last for long," she said, "and I'd hate for us to pretend. I think that's sick—when people pretend."

He doodled mentally. "What's wrong with pretended love in the absence of anything better?" he asked her and himself. He was playing with her.

"I should hate that."

"In the case of compassion, isn't it better to pretend to compassion than to express your indifference?"

"No, *non*, no, it would be better to be true to your feelings."

"Even to appear cruel?"

"Yes. Because it wouldn't be as cruel as the pretence."

"But sometimes you can be so neurotic that your true feelings—the way you want to feel—can't get through—when you're all hung up. Why not act the way you want to feel, until the hang-up passes."

"Once love is gone it never comes back."

"What about when you're angry—you mightn't feel loving then but love hasn't gone. Or when you feel hopeless—that passes and love comes back."

"Real love is always there and it never goes away."

They sat thinking in the fast methedrine silence.

"I don't want you ever to be false to me," she said, "and I don't think that we are neurotic."

He didn't usually talk like this about these things. The methedrine allowed him—his words breaking out like fowls through a broken fence.

They listened to the lute music, sitting cross-legged facing each other, with the methedrine singing through them.

"Soothe me," he said.

He lay his head on her lap. She put her hand down his shirt and rubbed his back.

"Come to bed," she said, "where I can properly soothe you."

They moved over to the bed in the corner of the cabin. The lantern burned a soft temple light. They undressed each other and stood naked, their hands touching each other. They kissed. Naked, he held her breasts and she took his penis in both her hands, holding his testicles tight. He became submissive to her touch. She responded, pulling him down gently to the bed, leading him by his swelling penis. In the lantern light the logs of the cabin wall rippled up to the roof. She held him tight in a kiss. He moved his head down to her breasts. She stroked him—pressed him against her breasts—nuzzled his hair. Then they petted in an erotic calm.

Then she whispered: "Give me your knife". He did not hear her clearly and shifted his head. "Give me your knife," she whispered. With an erotic trembling he reached across to his clothes beside the bed and unstrapped the knife from the belt and gave it to her.

In the lantern light he watched her strap it around her naked neck. The black bone handle of the heavy knife hung down between her young heavy breasts. She looked up at him, holding out her arms to him. She took him to her, pulling him over on to her, the knife coming hard against her skin pressing hard into her breasts. They rolled hard with the knife between them, clamped in a kiss. He felt the bucking and rearing of desire. They writhed and he felt the pleasure of the knife hurting. Swept by her deft sexuality. The knife like another penis. Her penis? Or did he have two? Or was it their penis? They rolled with the rearing desire.

Then he pulled back away from her, looking at the black leather strap and the black bone knife hanging from her neck against the soft white skin. The knife had left its imprint on her breast. She was his girl with his knife strapped to her. In the flickering of the lantern he grew dominant. He moved to her aware suddenly of how much bigger he was than she. She stared at him, her hands on his thighs, and then lay back wide, the knife lying against her body. He reached down touching her breasts and touching the knife. He pushed down on the knife tenderly hurting her, and then came down on her, entering her. She was his woman and the knife she had strapped to herself was his knife. She was his sexual liege, she lay back and wrapped her arms and legs around him in a gesture of total surrender.

"Have me," she said, laying there wide, the knife biting into her.

Later he went to piss. He stood cold, shivering in the winter damp grass. The knife was in his awareness but he did not bother with it intellectually. It had played a part in a wondrous pleasure. He went back into the cabin, wiping his wet feet on the blanket. He huffed out the lantern.

Crawling in beside her he again felt the knife between her breasts, as he held to her for warmth. They both lay electrically awake but unspeaking, the methedrine humming through the wires of their minds. They remained embraced throughout the night. He felt the knife during the night but did not wonder about it. They slept and made love again sometime early in the morning, sometime before dawn. They slept some more. She took the knife off sometime after that. In the morning when the sun was up the knife was beside them on the floor.

When he rose he strapped it back onto his belt.

That day they built an outdoor fire from stones and an old iron grid, carrying sand from the beach for the fire bed.

On Friday they went to a party in the city. A packed, three-storey terrace house. People they both knew. In jeans, drinking from bottles of beer and in one room the clandestine sweetness of pot. The constant, heavy rock beat. He moved restlessly from room to hallway to stairs to room. He knew that she was in the front room, or at least that was where he sensed she was. He wanted to talk to her but he resisted. They had not come to the party to do that. He imagined her talking in her tough guarded manner. The heavy, constant rock beat followed him from room to room. They were from another place and he felt it. They had detached themselves from the city for a while and re-entry was not a simple matter. He felt a distance from the city. Perhaps it was the distance he enjoyed in a mild sort of way. He was not alien. It was that the experiences and the tempo of their life at the cabin would not mesh with the wild agitation of the party. They were disengaged. They had been living alone and their social reflexes were slower and they weren't ready to change back yet.

Sally Fith came to him as he stood in the hall. Before, in the city, he had wanted now and then to get off with her. They sat down together in the hall.

She asked him about the life down at the cabin.

"It's a good life," he said, "but I'm frightened to say how good or to talk about it for fear the gods will take it from me." People stepped over them and around them and he felt as if they were sitting undiscovered while people passed by looking for them.

"Painting?"

"No—I've done a little sketching now and then. Essentially I'm doing nothing. I went there to do essentially nothing."

"Money?"

"Haven't bothered to calculate—we're still eating. Anne looks after all that."

"Is she hung up about the baby?"

"She doesn't talk about it. It's gone—finished. I think she'd talked it all out of herself before she met me."

"Anderson's around somewhere," Sally said tiredly.
"So what? He's finished with her. Is he finished with you?"
She gave her bitter wry smile. "Ex-husbands never finish with you. And Anderson always keeps sniffing around his old bitches."
He wanted Sally at times but she frightened him. She was older and had an analytical toughness. She wasn't aware she frightened him and therefore could not ease him nor could she turn the fear to a sexual excitement.
He felt his knife.
"Look at my knife," he said to her, pulling it from his pocket by the strap.
"A knife?"
"Yes, for hunting and carving."
"You don't hunt."
"I don't carve either—except I carved our names on a tree. In a heart with an arrow through it."
"How romantic."
He tossed the knife in his hand with short tosses.
"Are you and Anne having a serious thing?"
"Not really . . . not in the 'I am in love' sense but perhaps in other ways."
"The old ambiguity—you 'love' her in *your own way*—your private definition. But of course she thinks you 'love' her in *her way*."
He tightened. "No it's not like that—it's all understood. We understand the situation." He was uncomfortable. He didn't like to talk about his life in this analytical way. "Perhaps sometimes—I'm speaking hypothetically, not about Anne and me—sometimes ambiguity might be useful. Perhaps it's needed sometimes so that two people can get what they want from an affair."
"Roger! You're capable of the most miraculous rationalisations."
"I wasn't speaking about Anne and me. We understand each other."
"It'll be the first relationship in the world where both

people have."

"God I hate the word 'relationship'—you and the others use it all the time."

"We have so many . . ." she said drily.

"I want to show you my knife," he said again, opening out the blades.

"It has two blades, see?" He cut the floor.

"Why did you get it?"

"It has a needle, tweezers, a bottler opener, a can opener, and a corkscrew."

"Ooooh," she grinned.

"If you don't appreciate it I'll put it away," he said with mock injury.

"No—go on—I'm fascinated," her chin rested on her hand—one finger on the side of her face—she was looking at him, not the knife.

"I can see that you're not interested."

"I don't feel anything about knives."

"I felt I needed one." He closed it up.

"Probably an important male symbol. Painters always doubt their masculinity."

"For God's sake!"

"Just an impression I have."

He didn't want analysis. This always got between them before they could get off. He remembered then, the love-making with Anne and the knife. Sally could tear that apart with Freudian zeal. People were always unloading heaps of analysis onto his mind. He never knew what to do with it.

Sally put her hand on his neck, her fingers under his ear.

"You don't need any symbols, my sweet," she said. "Let's go upstairs and find a bed." She took his hand and kissed the side of his face.

He nearly took the easy way out and went but he sensed that it would be one of those unfortunate fucks where indifference on his part would cause it to finish messy and cold in an uncomfortable shared bed. And there was Anne.

"No Sally, not tonight. I don't feel good." He realised that he probably couldn't have anyway. He felt as closed up as the knife.

"WHAT ARE YOU doing this morning?" Anne asked, her mouth against his ear.

This morning. He rolled over and looked through the cabin window and saw the morning. An empty day before him. A free day or an empty day? He see-sawed.

He lay back, his fingers behind her neck, in her hair.

"I'll clean my knife," he said. "Today, I'll clean my knife."

"I'll watch."

He smiled at her. "You just want to watch me clean my masculinity symbol."

She frowned, puzzled. "Who said that was what it is?"

He laughed and didn't tell her.

"It's just your knife," she said. "It's nothing more than Roger's knife."

He rose, warmed some water and washed.

After breakfast he looked in the shed where he'd seen a whetstone. He took some oil and cotton waste and and steel wool and went to sit on a flat rock in the sun.

He used the steel wool to clean off the rust which had formed from the oystering. He made the steel clean, cool, and smooth to touch. He cleaned out the grit in the blade slots with a match stick twirled with waste. He oiled the knife lightly, rubbing the bone handle until it gleamed.

She lay on a blanket nearby in the sun and watched.

He spat on the whetstone and sharpened. He started at the circular smearing of the spittle and carborundum, whirling like a universe. After a while he tested the sharpness with his thumb and by slicing a blade of grass.

He oiled the joints, opening and closing the implements until they clicked free and tight and snapped out firmly. Finally inspecting the knife, he held it for a few seconds in his hand enjoying the weight of it and the shape, enjoying its existence. Then he buckled it back to his belt.

He looked at her lying on her back, her knees up, her dress bunched around her hips her legs apart to allow the sun to warm her. She was smiling to him. He let the knife fall to his thigh and wiped his hands on his jeans. He went over to her, kneeling down beside her and taking her in his arms. They made love in the sun on the grass.

A breeze made it too cool to stay there after they had finished and they went inside. She made coffee with milk.

"SO, MY SWEET GIRL, the knife is gone. And you are going too." Outside the city stood around, as if watching.

She drank down most of the glass of white wine.

"Yes, I'm going," she said. "Does it hurt you?"

"Yes, I'll miss you. It hurts." He was careful not to overstate his feelings.

"But you weren't ever involved in it. It was a passing thing for you. Everything passes, you say."

"All things pass."

"All things pass. I think we can have something better now between us, on a new and different basis, something less restricting on you, and because of that it will be freer and better."

Twenty-year-olds were *too much.* At times like this they were just *too much.*

"Why? Because it will be non-sexual?"

"No. It needn't be that—if you still want me—but because we won't be living together and constantly around each other—you won't have to take me into consideration."

He looked at her. She looked away.

"We can still go to bed together," she said, without looking at him. "If you still want me."

He said nothing. He sipped his scotch. Should you sip it? Should you throw it down like in the Wild West?

"You know what happened?" she asked.

"No . . what happened?" he poised for a surprise.

"When I found that the knife and the coat had gone—that very minute—it began to rain from a sunny sky."

Oh, no.

She came over to him and kissed him on the forehead. Then she went to the sink. She threw the dregs of her drink out and rinsed the glass, standing it upside down on the sink to drain.

"I'm going to get my gear and then I'll go."

He nodded. There were things he could say and some he wanted to say but he didn't. He had subsided. He shouldn't become mixed up with twenty-year-olds. With twenty-year-olds one was a father. A teacher. An oracle. A psychiatrist. A model. A priest. A reference book. A mentor. An ever-present refuge in times of real or imagined strife. It was tiring. Not because they took much which was of value but because of the demand from them for these roles. They gave you gifts—verbal and material gifts were constantly being laid at your feet. They were all undeserved gifts. Undeserved gratitude was the sourest of human profferings. One of the most difficult to turn away.

She came back down the stairs.

She was crying.

She came over to him and kneeling down beside the chair she put her face on his arm.

"I don't want to go, Roger. I really don't want to go."

He put his arms around her and said: "Sweet girl."

"I don't want to go."

"Don't go then—don't go."

"I was being stupid. I wanted to test you or something," she cried. "I couldn't leave you."

He looked across the kitchen at the Ajax, the Fab, the Lux, the Steelo. Outside the broom, the bucket, the tray, the brush, and the mop.

"Don't cry. You stay. We'll go on as we were."

"I won't bug you," she said. "I'm not possessive. I won't get like this again, I'll just be here when you need me." She held to him tightly and cried.

Twenty-year-olds were always softer and more susceptible than they pretended. And they didn't believe a lot of what they said. He'd forgotten that. You forget things for your own purpose. Anyhow, what the fucking hell.

What Can You Say?

WHEN I FIRST MET Jimmy I was nothing. Not that I'm claiming that I'm much now, but then I was nothing. I'd been a sales clerk for this big car firm and one day I just left. It is a long story and it doesn't seem to matter much now. It all had to do with the double-talk and "duplicity"—Jimmy's word—not only about my work but about the phoney way my mother and father and I lived. And about the way I was with Marj—telling each other we loved each other when we were just hanging around together out of habit—it would have gone on for the rest of our lives if I hadn't got out. At first I wrote to Father and Mother after I left home but I don't now. They kept trying to get me back to work and back home so I don't tell them where I live now. Marj evidently went hysterical but about two months later she was going out with a fellow who lived up the street from me. He can have her.

Well, I walked out on it all. I had this money saved up in the bank—to get married. I really did. $800. The money's gone now but in a way I'm glad.

I rented a flat at Kings Cross (the full bit) but I soon realised that I was being robbed, or at least, Jimmy pointed it out. I moved to Surry Hills in a room near the Vanity Fair Hotel where some of Jimmy's mates lived. Terri, Bernie, Teller and Anne and others. It's half the price and you don't get overcharged at the delicatessens the way you do at the Cross. But at first I lived in this flat at the Cross and I lived there for about four weeks. I met people in coffee shops and pubs, including a couple of queers who I promptly pissed off. I was very square then.

One day I went to a pub called the Royal George where beatniks go. I was living on my bank and didn't have much to do with myself. I'd usually get up about ten or eleven—sometimes not until lunch time. I'd go for a swim somedays or go to a movie or read a magazine. Must have read two million magazines. I joined the library—the one in the park.

They had racks of magazines.

Well, I went to the Royal George Hotel mainly out of curiosity. But I was sort of attracted to it as well. I was bored too. I was free but I was bored. Let's face it, until I left home I'd been working since school and every hour of my time seemed to be fairly full with Marj, squash, parties, television, the beach and so on. But now that I'd left all that to be free I found I was bored. Sometimes I'd go to sleep in the afternoons while I was reading and I'd wake up with gritty eyes and sweat and no energy. I wouldn't know what time it was. I'd feel so empty and tired and I'd just lie there dozing and waking and dozing in the dim room. I'd feel so empty. When I would be coming out of an afternoon movie I'd see people coming out of offices hurrying to go somewhere. I'd see people drinking in pubs after work and I knew that I had no time called "after work" and I knew that I had no after work-mates. Sometimes this was OK with me and other times it depressed me. Somedays life would be so dull that the most exciting thing that would happen to me was to eat a meal in a cafe or pull myself off in my room.

When I went to the George there was hardly anyone around. I suppose it was early for people to get there. I started to read a book I'd bought at the newsagent. Then a fellow with a beard came over to me and said: "Is Miller out in paperbook now?"

I said: "What? Who's he?"

"Henry Miller—the book you're reading."

"Oh, this book," I said, looking at the cover. "I just picked it up at the newsagents. I didn't look to see who wrote it."

The fellow with the beard seemed to think this was *very funny*. I knew he wasn't queer because of his beard but I was on guard because I didn't know if he was going to send me up or whether he was going to bite me for a drink. But he sat down and told me a few things about Henry Miller. Evidently Miller is bigtime. And then this fellow bought me a beer, so I guessed he was OK. He asked me who I was and where I came from. He said his name was Jimmy. It turned out that he was what he called an "anarchist" and he spent hours telling me about it because he said that I was an anarchist although I didn't know it.

He said he was a tutor in sociology at the university. I didn't believe him at first because he looked pretty rough.

He talked like a lecturer sometimes. He said that a person who fought against authority was an anarchist.

"It doesn't matter whether it's a dictator or a boss or the beloved majority, it is still an imposition on you—you're being pushed around. That's why anarchists are against democracy and the boss-worker situation."

Jimmy said that the only thing that had to be obeyed was reason—not the counting of heads or the fact that someone owned the shop where you worked.

It was Jimmy talking like this that made me realise that I was nothing. I probably would have said I was for the Australian way of doing things but when I heard him talking I realised I knew nothing. Nothing. I didn't know how to talk to him. Of course it was a sort of hero-worship from the start.

When Jimmy would turn to me and say: "Well, what do you reckon?" I would know that I had nothing to say but I often said something because I didn't want Jimmy to think I didn't have any brains. Not that I'm dumb. I just didn't know anything about the things he wanted to talk about.

Jimmy was really impressed with the fact that I'd walked out on everything but at the time I couldn't see why.

Jimmy took me to parties where I met other people including girls. And they'd talk to you. Jimmy was evidently a big man at these parties. Jimmy used to introduce me as a "bona fide primitive anarchist."

For quite a few parties I was fairly miserable, though. They were Jimmy's mates, not mine, and I had nothing much to say. I couldn't argue. I'd just listen. Sometimes when I did start to talk it would be so corny and out of place that they'd say: "Hold on, I want to get a drink, I'll be back." But they wouldn't come back. Sometimes there'd be dancing and I could dance OK.

Jimmy changed my ideas about sex. I remember at a party, him telling me that different people needed different sex lives and that the same person needed a different sex life at different times. In his slow, lecturer's voice, he said: "There are a diversity of personalities requiring a diversity of sexual relationships. This society says there is only one —marriage. All right so you want to raise a family—find a girl and go ahead. But it doesn't follow that you have to sleep with her only or she only with you."

I used to say that I couldn't understand how some of his friends could let other fellows get off with their girls. I said it would give me a pain in the gut.

But Jimmy would say: "You have to overcome jealousy. It's like bad temper—you learn to control it."

The first girl I became interested in was Wesley. She was beaut. But I was a dismal failure with her in bed. I felt as if I was a dead loss as far as sex was concerned. I thought I must be queer. It was about five days before I could make love to her properly. Jimmy made me read a few psychological books about it. I think I'd have gone off my head if he hadn't been around to explain it.

I began to read more books. I borrowed some of Jimmy's. I went to a few courses at WEA too. Those first four months with Jimmy were like a wild gallop. We stayed up all night sometimes just talking and drinking.

Then one day I was supposed to meet Jimmy in the pub and he didn't arrive. This was unusual for him. If he said he was going to be somewhere he'd be there. I waited a while wondering what to do and then I went to his flat.

I knocked. There was no answer. I knocked again and he yelled: "Who is it?"

I said: "It's me. Thomas."

There was a silence. I thought he might be with a woman and I should go away. But then he came to the door.

He looked shocking. He was pale and his eyes were bloody. He was staggering and shaking a little. I couldn't smell any drink.

"I'm a little pilled up," he said. "I'm a little sedated." He wasn't speaking clearly.

"You sick?" I asked.

We went into his book-filled mess of a bedroom. He rolled on to the bed.

"I'm sick in the head," he said.

"You've done psychology. Fix yourself up."

He snorted and mumbled: "Physician heal thyself."

I asked him what was wrong.

He looked nowhere and said: "Futility."

I sat on the edge of the bed and lit a cigarette.

"All is but a hollow, tinkling shell," he said.

"I don't follow you," I said.

As though he wasn't speaking to me or to anyone, and as though he was forcing himself to talk, he said: "All my rational life I have lived as an intellectual Arab in a mental tent on the border of two countries. The countries of futility and hope."

I had never heard Jimmy talk like this. I guess it was the pills he'd taken. I carefully ashed my cigarette on the bed post, wondering what to say.

"Why?" I was glad I could ask that.

"Why? Because. Because all people do or want to do is push someone around."

"Roll with the punch," I said, trying to be tough-minded. It was a thing he had often said to me.

"The world is staggering towards mass mental illness, or totalitarianism, or starvation or it will blow itself up. Or all three."

"Four," I said, wishing I hadn't.

Then I heard him crying. It was the first time I'd see a man cry. I sat still and thought how clumsy my brain was. Then I put my hand on the back of Jimmy's neck.

He cried for only about half a minute or so and I didn't do anything or say anything but left my hand on his neck.

Then he stopped and said: "There is a point, Thomas, a point, when your experience is wide enough and your grasp of reality such, that you feel you have either experienced the sweetest of joys and some of the deepest of misery, or that you can at least imagine these, and it is then that you see life as a succession of these joys and miseries spaced by petty, intermediate, dullness. The prospect of this no longer excites you. It just tires you. I'm tired."

His arm stuck out from the edge of the bed and his hand hung limp. He said in the same tired, forced voice: "It is like a party. It might be dull now or good now or you might be going to fight someone or get off with some girl, but the important thing is that you know what *can* happen and you know that if you stay something *will* happen, and that it will either excite you or bore you or do nothing to you. It's deciding when to leave the party—deciding when you've had enough."

I took my hand away. It was then I realised that he was talking about suicide. I still didn't know what to say.

I said: "You once said that things were self-justifying. That things don't have to be anything or mean anything. You said a good relationship with a woman was enough."

"That's irrelevant," he said, "except the part about the woman." He sounded as if he was correcting an essay.

Then I felt useless and irritated because I was useless. Because I didn't have any arguments to use against him. Then I thought that if anything made me want to stay alive it was being with Jimmy or Wesley. Both made me feel as though I was "living". But Jimmy wanted to die. This would mean that I would feel less alive—a bit dead. I resented that he didn't want to stay alive because of me.

Jimmy went to sleep. I went out and bought three bottles of beer. I drank and read and wandered about the flat. I tried to think about what he had said. I was dazed because until now Jimmy had always had the world licked. He had always had the answers. And now he was lying there knocked out with pills. It made me feel alone and uneasy. But I felt other things for him because he was my mate.

When he woke up he had a beer. We drank a bottle more and then went to the Greek's for a meal and then to the George, hardly saying anything to each other. I knew that it had been a bad, sad day for Jimmy. But I couldn't do anything. I didn't know what was happening to him. I don't think I was game enough to understand what he had said. I wanted to ask him but I didn't know how. I was worried because I didn't have anything to say to him. I had nothing to say that would make him feel OK. I wasn't a bloody priest. All I could do was stand there with him while we drank beers and be with him.

"No Birds Were Flying Overhead, There Were No Birds to Fly"

I ALWAYS LEAVE a funny personal mess in my desk-drawer. But they'll clean it out and throw it away gingerly —the poor puzzled things—sitting around saying: "She was odd, wasn't she?" I wonder what they'll think as they clean out my funny personal mess. Those peanuts, the forget-me-not pill, the methedrine, the letter from Mark in Canada. Will they read that? Of course they'll read it.

She paused to look at handbags in the shop window. The suede handbag. She went into the shop and asked to see it so that she could feel it. You can ask to see a bag but you can't ask to feel a bag.

"The quality is not what I expected, thank you for your trouble."

My voice is too modulated. That's why they won't employ me sometimes. I'm too Vogue-dressed and too radio-spoken and too actress-charming. Wouldn't it give you the shits. Blame mother.

They say: "You wouldn't be happy here. It's not a glamour job. We'd like very much to employ you on a higher level but we haven't a vacancy. You wouldn't be happy here. You'd be wasted."

"Oh, but I'd very much like the position. It does really appeal to me."

"You wouldn't like the job because it's below you. You wouldn't be happy here. You should really apply for a better position. We are sure that you wouldn't be happy here."

Why don't they give me a job instead of telling me what will make me happy—as if a job could ever make me stuffing happy. God almighty. What am I supposed to wear—hessian bags? And how am I supposed to talk—like a bus conductress?

She stopped at a bookshop. She browsed along the books, her fingers tripping over the gloss of the new books. She smelled the sauerkraut smell of the layers of printed words, compressed and unreleased between the new paper of the pages.

"Can I help you madam?"

"Would you have the Bodley Head Scott Fitzgerald, Volume Two?"

"Yes madam, I think we do. I shan't be a moment."

Does he realise he's serving the best-dressed bum in town.

"Here we are madam."

"Thank you. I'll take it."

"I'll have it wrapped for you."

"Thank you, place it on my account—Miss L. Henderson, Peter Street, Paddington.

Come on, Scott, let's have a drink. I really don't read as much as I think I read. But it is comforting to have a book and to know that you can read it if no one is around, or if you do not wish to speak to anyone, but do not on the other hand, wish to be left alone with your ants-nest mind. You can read a book but it can't read you. You can put it down and pick it up but it can't put you down and pick you up. A book is so suitably passive.

She went to the bar and to the red telephone. She began to dial Franny's number and then stopped. She went to the barmaid and ordered vodka and lime with ice.

"Could I have more ice please, heaps and heaps . . . lovely . . . ta."

She went to the phone and dialled Franny's number but as it went brrrr and brrrr she put it down and sipped her drink. Then went to the Ladies to piss.

Hot stepins. If I had a bigger bag to put them in I'd take them off and feel freer. My God darling how much freer do you want to be? Free to starve? Well, it'll be a telephone call to auntie. "Auntie sweetheart, may I borrow fifty dollars? I'm changing positions. Something more glamorous. Yes, Derek is getting me a position as a private secretary to one of the Ministers—Shipping or Defence or something. Overseas trips. Yes, that's right—overseas missions." Dear old auntie, she'll give.

She pissed, leaning forward, arms on her knees, huddling herself, holding her skirt with her elbows. Huddling in a cubicle with herself. Exactly the way she did when she was a little girl.

She went to the red telephone and dialled Franny's number and it went brrrr and brrrr and she sipped her vodka and lime and watched who entered the bar, through careless eyes that had watched many times before. She was conscious of the elegance of her stance.

"Franny? Look darling I've left that shithouse job. Couldn't bear it. Really intolerable."

"Why? But why for God's sake?"

"Couldn't stand it. Just couldn't stand it. Nothing dramatic. Couldn't stand them talking about their new shifts and blouses and shoes they buy at lunch-time when they've saved up enough to take them off lay-by. So ugly and shoddy. The people were all ugly and shoddy. The place sold ugly and shoddy things so they needed ugly and shoddy people to run the place. I could feel myself becoming ugly and shoddy—I really could, darling. You've no idea."

"But look sweet, this is the third time in six months. You can't go on doing it. It's not responsible."

"Responsible? What does that mean? Responsible—shit! I'm responsible to myself. I didn't like it and I wasn't going to stay. Is there anything you want me to pick up in town to take back to the flat?"

"Look, Louise, you can't just walk out on jobs like this. Let's have a talk tonight. Where are you now?"

"Fran. There is nothing, absolutely nothing, to talk about."

"What about the rent! Do I have to pay rent for another two months while you 'recover' from God knows what?"

"Fran, if you're going to be a shit about it then you be a shit. I paid you back all the rent from last time. I'm getting some money from auntie. If you're going to be a shit then I'm not talking to you. Bye. See you when I get home."

"But Lou . . ."

She put the red telephone down and ordered a vodka and lime. With her long fingernails she tore the wrapping from the Scott Fitzgerald, Volume Two.

"Ice please . . . heaps and heaps . . . thank you darling."

She rippled the pages and smelled the book.

She looked up and saw Marylou walk into the bar, eye make-up, no lipstick, flat shoes, suede handbag, Penguin book.

"Lo Louise."

She kissed Marylou and they squeezed each other carefully.

"Guess what, Louise, I've just taken a sickie."

"Guess what, Marylou, I've just walked out."

Marylou squealed.

"Yes, have a drink. A celebration."

"How divine. You like walking out, don't you? I'm going to do that next. I didn't wake up till eleven today. I've been getting later and later. I said bugger and went back to sleep. I'm really a midday-riser by nature and it's wrong for me to get up at eight to go to work. It's unnatural. But tell me. Tell me about walking out."

"Nothing dramatic darling. *Work* is against my nature. I just found the job too, too tiresome. God. When I left school I was eager enough for the money and I saw myself as private secretary and all that jazz. I really didn't think that I'd have to work for *years* for animals. I know now just how tiresome work really is."

"Let's go on the streets, Louise. It's the only way for us. No boss. No set hours. Just lying on our backs."

Marylou sighed, sipped her drink, looked at the Scott Fitzgerald, looked around the bar and sighed again.

"Have you told Fran you left the job?"

"I rang her just now. She's furious. She thinks she'll have to pay the rent for the next two months—she will, of course. I'm broke."

"She's just sorry she didn't walk out first."

"She said something about responsibility. What does that word mean, Marylou?"

"I don't know, I've never heard it before."

They sat on their stools, silent.

"Instead of going on the streets, Marylou, let's start a call girl racket. What would be wrong with a call girl racket?"

"I've thought of it hundreds of times. Every girl in the world must think about it at some time. I honestly don't know why more girls aren't doing it. I really can't."

"It's just a matter of getting set up."

"The way I see it is that it is just another sort of work, only there's less of it and it's better paid. And not dull. Could even be fun."

"Must meet some disgusting men though."

"You have to put up with disgusting men everywhere."

"The chief clerk—an animal called Nish at the last place—he literally perved all day. I mean he really did. And every remark was a dirty innuendo: 'Didn't you get enough sleep last night Miss Henderson?—only naughty girls don't get enough sleep.' He'd go on and on and on."

"Let's not talk about the bastards we've worked with. Let's not start."

"I honestly can't see anything wrong with the call girl deal. It'd be mainly business men and interstate people. You'd never see most of them again."

"I met a girl at a party who said she was in a deal. They

were paying her fifty dollars a night. But you had to do anything they asked. Businessmen."

"I couldn't imagine anything I wouldn't do, can you?"

"For fifty dollars I'd do anything."

"Dishonour before death."

"It's the sort of men that puts me off a bit."

"At least you'd expect that businessmen would have a bath everyday. That's something."

"If we could line it up would you be in it? I'm serious, Marylou. Would you?"

"Of course I would."

"All we need is a flat, a telephone, a few introductions. A couple of afternoons sitting in the lounge of the Menzies Hotel would be enough."

"God, I bet there are hundreds of fat old men dying for a good fuck—or a pervy fuck that they wouldn't get from their wives."

They ordered two more vodka and limes with plenty of ice.

"When did you leave the job?"

"About an hour ago."

"What did you tell them?"

"I didn't tell them anything. I just walked out. I just picked up my handbag and walked out. I lost two days' pay but what the hell."

"If we get set up there'll be no more of those starvation days before payday. Scratching money together for a bus fare. Looking around under the bed for cents. Gives me the shits."

"And no more coming into the bar hoping to find someone who'll shout you a drink."

"Are you really serious about the idea, Louise? Really?"

"Yes! It's just another kind of work."

"I'm not saying that there is anything wrong with it."

"Well, let's do it."

"Here's a toast to the end of those days before pay day."

"To the end of crawling to get a job, and to getting up late in the morning, and to no more pies for lunch, and no more laddered stockings."

Marylou touched her arm. She turned and saw Derek ponder into the bar. She saw him look to the far side and then to her. She turned to look at Marylou.

Marylou said: "Are you going to tell him? What will he say?"

"He won't mind. He's free and easy. I'll just tell him."

Derek said: "Hullo, why aren't you two at work? Robbing the economy again?"

She traced the cover design of the Bodley Head Scott Fitzgerald with her fingernail and said: "I've just walked out."

"No! Jesus wept. Not again."

"Look, before you two start, I'm off. Bye bye, Derek. I'll phone you later, Louise."

She watched Marylou skip out of the bar. She turned to Derek who was smiling, perplexed.

"But why? Jesus you're impossible. You're a foolish and impossible girl."

"They were tiresome people to work for, Derek."

"The world is tiresome but you don't just walk out of it. You learn to put up with it—to adjust."

"I don't think that it has to be tiresome. I'm certainly not going to learn to put up with it."

He laughed without much force. "Jesus wept."

He ordered drinks. "What are you going to do then? Become an anarchist or something?"

"Not exactly."

She looked down into the Bodley Head Scott Fitzgerald. She saw the seriphs of the typography and looked deep into the curls of the design.

"What are you going to do?"

"I'm not going to work. Not for them. Not for anyone like them."

"Well what are you going to do? You can't sit here drinking and reading Scott Fitzgerald for the rest of your life."

"Why not? It sounds OK to me."

Being a little girl was wearing starched dresses and having mummy brush your hair which smelt like water and sun. Everything was fresher then. My body was always clean and smelled sweet by itself. Without any deodorant. Bodies are like anything getting old—they smell and become stained and marked. Become shabby. My fingernails look young because they are young. Fingernails are self-renewing. But skin isn't. I think insides become smelly too.

"Hey, dreamy! What are you going to do? You know I can't keep you in the style to which you've been accustomed. What are you going to do?"

"Might go away to the country for a break. I'm tired of the city."

"And then what? That's just escape."

"I need a break."

"But how many jobs is this you've left in the last year? Four? It must be nearly four."

"This was the last. There is not going to be another."

"What are you going to do? What about Franny and the flat?"

"I've told Franny."

"What did she say?"

"She was furious."

"What are you going to do? You can't expect her to pay your rent again."

Derek can be tiresome. Derek is an orderly man. Derek is a cautious man. Derek has no fun. For Derek everything must be a step towards something else. It is—death. But he doesn't know it. A picnic with Derek is just a number of jobs to be done. It's never the picnic at any time—it's buying the food, it's packing the gear, it's finding the spot, it's lighting the fire, it's finding water, it's laying out the food, it's keeping away the flies, it's opening tins and bottles, it's watching your diet, it's watching your ulcer, it's packing up the gear, it's washing things, it's putting them in the car, it's traffic jams home. It's never fun. And there's never anything called the picnic that happens. Why do I bother with him?

Apathy. I couldn't be bothered breaking off with him. I can't be bothered bothering about him.

"If seven maids with seven mops,
Swept it for half a year,
Do you suppose, the Walrus said,
That they'd ever get it clear?
I doubt it, said the Carpenter,
And shed a bitter tear".

"What are you talking about? What do you mean?"

"I'm shedding a bitter tear."

"Listen, Louise, pull yourself together. What are you going to do, honey? Let's talk about it. I want to help you."

"If seven maids with seven mops . . ."

"Louise!"

"Look, Derek, let's talk about something else. Please, Derek. I'm tired of this subject. Talk about something else."

Anderson, How Can There Be a Baby and No Crying?

HE WAS MY HUSBAND for two years and therefore the way I see his life, the part he has lived so far, is sure to be twisted a little, but I'm sure only a little, by the fact that he left me and broke my heart.

I'm sure that it is twisted only a little because I am known for my detachment. Even during emotional turmoil I can analyse clearly. But I can feel too and I find it doesn't help me much to be able to analyse. It never really assuages the crying mind, but I think that it probably makes those long personal conversations—those outpourings of the heart—a little more bearable to dear friends who have to listen. A sound piece of analysis makes them feel they are getting something which could possibly be of value to *them* and not purely one's own sentimentality or self-pity. Some men have told me that my ability to analyse is unwomanly. Some simple men mistake it for coldness. I'm too verbal and it frightens them. But those who have found their way to my bed find that I am sensual as well as verbal. Sometimes this frightens them all the more.

But what my husband, Anderson Fith, could not accept, although the darling had the intelligence and understanding to realise that the verbal and sensual are not incompatible, was my maternity. I wanted children.

Of course it would be easy to say, as I did for a time, that he wanted his wife as a co-worker. Well, he got a co-worker. But in fairness I think now that deep down—not as deep as the bottom of his stomach, however—he wanted to have children too. And I'm not sure I understand what stopped him. Whatever barrier did stop him from making the step from *wanting* to *having,* I didn't break it. This was perhaps my failure. God knows I've got my failings too and I don't think he alone was responsible for the disintegration of our marriage.

I remember the first time I asked Anderson for a child. "There you go," the anti-verbalists will say, "children are not asked for, they happen—they come about." Or something happens below the clumsiness of words. Well, I say this is romantic piffle. Words can be just as human and as soft as a touch or kiss—but in many cases less ambiguous. I sometimes think that people who fear words when dealing with emotional matters fear facing their own confusion. They make me sick.

I remember details. It was a summer afternoon and I was wearing a kimono and nothing else. In summer I often wear no underclothes and go barefoot around the house. My journalist brother brought the kimono back from Japan for me four years before when I was eighteen. But I had grown some since I was eighteen—around the breasts and hips especially, to my advantage, I think. The kimono featured this advantage. Anderson was reading and I was writing a report. The temperature was high enough for me to become aware of the heat of my body and the silk of the kimono against it and the cool dampness of sweat under my arms. As I was writing I became aware that I would like to make love. Towards this end I prepared two glasses of brandy and ice and gave one to Anderson. As I did I leaned over him and he felt my breasts swinging free under the kimono. We didn't finish the brandies.

It began as languorous love-making with waves of intensity and troughs of calm. During the calm there were long eye-caresses and lazy words—almost becoming conversation (yes, we even talked during love-making!). And it became conversation because a feeling caught me and I looked at Anderson and wanted to have a baby for us. I said so. I said that we'd talk about it after but that I felt it in my loins now. That we should begin, one day soon, loving for babies. I knew it was perfectly right to feel this and to say this then, at that time. But Anderson did not respond.

He was playful and grinned. I wanted him to be serious and recognise the deepness and importance of what I was saying and feeling. More than that I wanted him to have the same feeling at the same time as I. But he grinned and said: "You're feeling maternal are you? Well, mother me. I'm not sharing you with any squawking brat." The words entered my mood like nails.

The disharmony of it was sad. Of course, I know that two people, no matter how close are not always in harmony. But I thought I knew, I was so sure that at that time, at just that moment, about a baby, we were in harmony. It came as a dazing thing to me to realise that we weren't. Anderson did not feel the disharmony but it was like sand between my legs. When we had finished I was not restful or released but hot, and I rolled away from under him and lay away thinking about why this harmony did not exist.

We talked about the baby in the warm, burnt-toast rationality of the breakfast table, a day or so later. But he said that first, we could not afford it, and second, he wanted to go overseas in a year or so and the baby would be a hindrance. Oh yes, and he said I would not be able to enjoy the trip if we had a baby. We should wait a couple of years, at least until we had returned. I realised, but did not admit, that I didn't want his baby now. I so feared my maternal urge that after conversation I took special attention not to miss a day with the pill. He would have thought a pregnancy was intentional or a Freudian error—he blamed me for my Freudian errors. After that day we did not talk about babies again but perhaps he felt it lying underneath the surface of our loving—like a crocodile? How horrible.

It is impossible to say that from that hot unharmonious love-making on that hot afternoon began the disintegration of the marriage. I suppose that sometimes it is possible to say that event A or event B was the first event in the breakdown of a relationship. I'm not that confident. But it was in the time around then and after that, that we started to break. I sensed it and would in the dark of the night in bed, ask Anderson if something was troubling him or wrong with us. I would ask him if he was tired of making love to me. He would just say: "No, don't be silly." I would believe him and it makes me sore now to think how I was deceived—both by him and myself—and how I allowed myself to believe his reassurances. Oh, the damage two people can do by denying the truth of each other's intimate observations! I would detect that he was not loving me with the same intensity. You can tell, especially after the first suspicion. You can feel how he handles you and how his body is lying on you . . . oh, everything . . . little things . . . some below conscious perception. Well, I would say that I didn't think he was loving me with the same feeling and he would deny this. He would become angry about it. And then I would doubt my judgement, doubt my body and feelings. I would say to myself: "You're becoming neurotically hypersensitive. You fear loss of Anderson's love and you're demanding that Anderson display more affection to reassure you and, because he doesn't, your fear misinterprets it as declining affection." Perhaps my feelings were changing but I didn't want them to. The terrible, terrible, damaging thing was that he *was* losing his feelings for me. I was correct and he was lying.

Then about three months after that vivid, hot afternoon, Anderson came home after midnight, ruffled and agitated. I was reading. I waited for him to say something about his obvious agitation. I sensed too that something was going to be said. He sat down in a bedroom chair facing away from me. He hooked a leg over an arm of the chair and his other foot tapped in a quick, unsettling way—no beat, just tapping. I wanted to say: "For God's sake stop tapping your foot."

Still looking away from me he said: "I love another woman." I put the book down calmly enough, marking the page, and then began to shake. Then the silly questions about who and why. And then the crying. He couldn't comfort me. I was blacked-out by that aloneness which comes when you are rejected by the only person who is close to you. That ugly aloneness. It goaded me to hate, then to despair and then to subjugation. I abused, then I pleaded, and then I offered anything—to do anything to regain what could not be so regained.

He was very willing to give details. Of course he wanted to tell someone about it.

I asked for details which were so painful as to be almost impossible for me to receive. Curiosity is a heartless feeling. It pushed aside my emotional self-protection like a school bully and demanded the details. She was married with two children. They had been talking about her leaving her husband. Their sexual life was "supremely good." Ugh. And, he said, with a sickening tone of importance and responsibility, he wanted to take the children as well and raise them as his own. You can see how this bit into me. I was being rejected not only as a lover but also as a mother for his children. He preferred second-hand children. But I won't go into that. I became derisive.

Well, I packed and went to live with my girlfriend, Terri. She was soothing and consolatory. She said little, listened, would caress me at night when I cried, would rub my back when I was blue, and she warded off unwanted visitors.

When I had recovered slightly I determined, for pride and other reasons, to rush back to normal living and this haste caused me to misjudge myself and I forced my spirit too hard. I found myself in that most miserable situation of going to bed with someone who is wonderful, and who could have conceivably been an important person to me, but because of emotional ill-timing being unable to allow my painful heart to move let alone give it to someone. I would feel afterwards like a madam with my heart and my body as child prostitutes. At that time I should have been home reading, or on a cruise, or drunk—not in bed with a man—not yet.

But, regardless of these mistakes and this rush, I recovered. I recovered to the point where I answered the telephone in Terri's flat one day and a woman said: "Mrs Fith? This is Marjorie Summers . . . I have . . . been associated with your husband . . . I'm sorry to bother you but I would like to have a talk with you if I may . . ." And I didn't drop the telephone.

I knew who she was and I was perplexed to hear her using the word "associated." Given that it was partly a problem of two people communicating in such a situation, it was also, I felt, an acknowledgement by her that something had happened that made her prefer the vague formality of "associated" to the words like "involved with" or "living with." She proposed we have coffee and I agreed.

Anderson had not gone to live with her. She told me how she had spent long nights convincing her husband that their marriage was finished and that she wanted to take the children and live with Anderson. The husband had agreed in despair. But then Anderson had said no he couldn't—he couldn't take the children. He had his career. He wanted to go overseas. (I registered this with an internal smile of superior understanding.) Anderson had wanted her to come with him—but not the children.

"I couldn't leave my husband *and* my children," she said. "I couldn't. I just couldn't. My marriage wasn't terrible, you know. It wasn't that bad. It was just lifeless. I love Anderson but I also love my children. I couldn't give everything up for him. He couldn't understand this."

I was prettier than she—and emotionally whole. She was

in the middle of her misery and so, in the situation, I was dominant. I was as comforting as I could be but I was, I'm afraid, a little bitchy too.

I said: "I thought Anderson loved your children. He told me how he played with them—they called him 'Hans Christian Anderson' and would rush to the door when he came." I was probing but flouting my information at the same time. She didn't appear to feel it. Anderson had had to tell me these delightful little details. Oh, a man with intelligence and perception can be so masterful at emotional demolition. Fires will burn on the site for a long time.

"Yes, they do love him," Marjorie Summers said. "He had a gentle manner and he was so playful. He is more playful with children than any man I know. It's so rare. My husband was never interested in the children. Anderson invented games and stories for them and really, I sometimes felt ignored because he spent more time with the children than with me."

She stared at her coffee and then with tear-glinted eyes said: "Why doesn't he want them? Why didn't he take me and the children together? They are a part of me. I'd do anything for him. I'd work so that we could all go overseas. But I can't leave my children."

I was of no help to her. I couldn't explain why he wouldn't take the children, nor could I tell her the magic method of making him. I think she expected me to know a magic way. That we expect magic from another human is amazingly primitive, be we do.

So I heard later that they had completely finished their affair. Then contact between Anderson and me resumed slightly for a month or so. He might have been toying with the idea of reconciliation or he may have been filling the gap between Marjorie Summers and the next affair. He told me how he had sent the Summers' children bicycles as parting presents and how the husband had sent them back.

We didn't discuss reconciliation. I was wary and self-protective and I think this showed in my careful remoteness. After we had both realised that there was almost no life in the relationship we did not persist with our meetings.

I found a satisfactory, if not thrilling, friend who could talk and love entertainingly. He had that nice sense not to load the relationship with demands it would not carry.

I next met Anderson in Pitt Street, arm in arm, head to head, with a girl I did not know. She had long black hair, untrimmed but well brushed, which reached the small of her back. She wore no shoes. She was dumpy and wore sunglasses. By appearance she was beat. But she was wearing an expensive, light-grey, Italian style flannel suit and had on a hand-made brass bracelet. A chic change from copper. She had clean ears too. He introduced her as Anne—no surname. He was grinning widely and mischievously in a way that I knew meant something like "I have a surprise for you which is not necessarily funny but is interesting." I ignored the grin, thinking that it referred to Anne's beatness. But as we talked I realised that Anne was either very plump indeed—or she was pregnant. Then as she twisted restlessly I saw that she was pregnant. The observation slapped me as it passed by.

By the time I had arrived back at the flat I was disturbed. I was disturbed by the idea of Anderson fathering a child with another woman. A woman who seemed, by style of life, to be so different from me as to be frustratingly beyond competition. I told myself this quite frankly. I was further disturbed that I could still be disturbed by Anderson. I walked aimlessly about the flat saying the incantation, "c'est la vie," and trying not to cry. I then decided to burn the fever out of me by exposing myself fully to the painful heat of it. I rang Anderson and arranged to have a beer with him .

"What is she?" I asked with a pretended nonchalance. "Angry, beat or square?"

He laughed and drank from his beer. "She is unique. She had the freedom of a beatnik, the sensibility of an angry, and perhaps you could say she has the old-world charm of a square."

"A personality smorgasboard," I said, "and by the shape

of things I would say it is a serious liaison." It was a tired pun and Anderson missed it.

"It is. It is. Anne is a very wonderful girl. We are both in it very seriously."

"Where did you meet her?" I asked.

"At a party. She dances like a native."

"You must be very sure of the relationship to have begun a family. I gather she *is* pregnant."

"Hell no—I mean, yes, she is pregnant—but no, I'm not the father. She was three months gone when I met her. That's the beatnik or native coming out in her—the father shot through and she doesn't give a damn. I'm the step-father, in a sense."

He said this with the same tone of pride and importance that I recalled him using when talking about the children during the Summers affair. But the fact that it was not his child relieved that stupid, romantic part of me which still persisted in its feelings for Anderson despite all that I had told it and done against it.

He said Anne was living with him and he was keeping her.

"Are you going to raise the baby?" I asked.

"Yes, I'm very fond of Anne, and the baby is part of her. That's if things work out—and I'm sure they will."

"Were you attracted by her pregnancy?"

He acted as if he was surprised by this question.

"I don't think so. It was novel but I was attracted to her —as a person. Look, I may be a bastard but I'm not a pervert." He laughed. "I can still make love to her you know—up to the eighth month. I'm reading a book about babies. I'm almost an expert on it. Anne refuses to read books about it. She thinks it's natural."

Of course, Anderson would become an expert on it.

"Still, a pregnant woman must be a change for you. Piquant, isn't that the word?"

"You're becoming too much the sexual sophisticate," he said.

"So you really do intend to keep the baby?"

"Yes, I think so. I had other plans as you know but I think—it's bloody hard to say—but, yes, Anne and I will raise the baby as our own. The baby is important to Anne and Anne is important to me."

We got quite drunk that night and Anderson placed his hand warmly on my thigh as we drove home. I let it rest there for the evidence in it that Anderson was still attracted to me. But I gathered enough control to avoid becoming drunkenly involved with him in bed. I couldn't face involvement with him and that is what it would have meant. Not with him living with a pregnant girl. Not the three and a half of us. It was not my sort of mess.

I kept a mental file of information about Anderson and his incipient family, gathered at parties and from mutual friends. As far as I could see I did this not because of any driving emotional concern for Anderson—the slight resurge was a passing thing—but because of a perverse interest in the child and the effect it would have on Anderson. The birth became one of the handful of expectations which are intriguing enough to justify living on in the world. I suppose I felt, as someone remarked at a party, that I was in someway related to the family.

I rang Anderson the day after the birth.

"Congratulations, father," I said drily.

"It's a boy," he said. "They're both doing well—arrived at midnight almost on the stroke."

"Well, you've got a family started now," I said. "What is he going to be named?"

"Well, it is not going to be like that," he said. "We've arranged for it to be adopted. I think that's the best thing."

Yes, I thought, of course, yes of course.

"We talked about keeping it," he went on, "but I'm going overseas next year and Anne's coming with me. We agreed that the baby would be a drag. Remember it wasn't my baby—I mean it's different. Anne wanted to keep it—she's cut up about it—but sense prevailed. We can start from the beginning now." There was just that slight trace of defensiveness.

"We'll wait until we come back from overseas," he said.

And I thought but did not say: "You are a self-deceiving bastard, Anderson Fith, a self-deceiving bastard—or I'm a poor, twisted woman."

Across the Plains, Over the Mountains, and Down to the Sea

"IT WAS THE ROAD on which Cindy and I had driven. We drove from a long way inland on a hot day to the coast. We drove the car on to the beach and swam naked. It was that road in the dream."

"Was this trip of special importance to the affair? What was its significance?"

"Oh yes. Yes, it was a climax. It symbolised everything. It symbolised the leaving of a hot, dusty and choking marriage for the clean, free sea."

"I want you to describe the trip and I want you to free-associate on the dream."

How do you describe to a psychiatrist when you are blocked by overlapping grief and jubilation. Grief from having lost perfection, and the jubilation from having had it. God, we loved then. It may have been neurotically doomed but god it felt right. I feel tears about it now. But I do not want to cry. Cindy released me. I don't mean from marriage—I had left that myself—but from a living numbness. She was coming alive out of childhood and I was coming alive out of this numbness from an anaesthetised marriage.

The marriage wasn't bad in the hostile yelling way. I've told you about the marriage. We could never admit to each other that there was anything wrong with the marriage because we were supposed to be perfectly suited and had to live out all our private proclamations about how superior our marriage was to those around us. We had to live out our marriage propaganda. And I left my wife then, not understanding why, and Cindy left me later not understanding why.

At the time of the trip Cindy and I had been together a month. We had to go inland, where a friend's book was being launched.

"You use the word 'inland'."

"Yes."

In-land. Within-land.

"Oh yes—I see."

Well, at the launching we drank champagne, toasted, danced and cheered and sang. It was the first book by the first of our friends to publish a book. I remember holding Cindy and feeling the fire coming from her hot body. Everything was hot and delirious. It was a raging "inland" heat during the day and like the heat of the hot coals at night.

"Tomorrow we go home. We'll drive that 360 miles straight to the sea," I said.

"Yes. Please. Let's do that," she said. She could be as bright eyed as a child.

"We will rise early at daylight and drive to the sea, across the plains, over the mountains, and down to the sea. I know a road over the mountains off the highway which is shorter."

"Yes, we'll do that. We'll swim naked."

Drunk, we made love in the motel. I tasted the salty sea juices which came from her. I sucked them from her to my parched river bed. Those juices left a taste that I can never swallow away. They were of the whole world.

We rose to a squinting hot sun. We had fruit juices, grilled lambs fry and bacon, and very cold milk. We ate in bed. I saw Cindy's teeth against the milk. Very white, perfect. Then we showered together and we made love in the shower under water, standing up.

The day was very hot and we sweated as we packed the car. With bad love the packing of the car is the greatest irritation of all. For us it was the best of all games.

We drove then along the blue highway. There was a shimmer by ten. The bush had that screech of hot insects, as through burning to death. And there was a smell of scorched foliage and drying mould. Cindy looked at the shimmer of the highway and said, "The road is dancing with us." She said the sticking bitumen was a-kissing at our tyres.

We talked about how love was not our word. Not the word we would use. We would escape its fouled-up connotations. We wanted a new word for what we had. We celebrated our feelings by eating peanut butter sandwiches from a country store. They tasted as no other sandwiches have ever tasted to me. And we had a can of cold beer.

We reached the mountains by two. They were cooler but still the sun was hot. They had more moisture. I supposed they were protected by the thicker growth. It was cooler because of the moisture. I drove on the winding road over the mountains. Further on I knew the shorter road which went to the coast. It was a stony and unsealed road with trees which touched overhead. The road jumped the car about because of the speed we drove over the stones—we were impatient for the sea. It is not a well-known road, no other cars passed us. It was our road. We saw the sea from the top of a rise in the stony road. Cindy squealed and pointed and hugged me. For all the driving she smelled as clean as the shower.

We drove down the last of the stony road with the dust choking up through the car. Bouncing, we came to the sealed road and the coast.

The car sang along after the stones. We drove fast to the sea, across the grass and on to the deserted beach. It was about four. We pulled the clothes off each other. Damp with sweat. Her body was just out of adolescence. Breasts only slightly larger than my own. We ran naked into the sea. Holding hands, into the cold sea. I remember the sea, cold and swirling around my penis. I felt enlivened.

It was as if the journey had been a *passing through*—360 miles across the hot plains, over the moist mountains, through the tunnel of trees, and down the sea. We had been together a month then. It was the leaving of my stultifying marriage for the clean free sea.

But do you know something—and it is this which upset me so much since I saw you last. Cindy and I have only been separated two years. The other night I was talking to her at a party and I told her that I had dreamed of the trip. She smoked in her new careless way and said, "What trip?" I said the trip from inland, over the mountains, and down to the sea. We made it. Remember?

"No," she said, "I don't remember it."

I went out of the party and on to the balcony of the house and wept.

I'm crying now.

"That's all right. When you're ready, we'll analyse the dream."

Rambling Boy

HE CAME OVER TO me, parting the bushes of the party to reach me.

"I met your wife," he said. "I met her in New York with SANE."

His American voice was like fingertips on my face. But my wife. Robyn. My wife? Why did the word still pinch me. Now. She was not my wife except in law but perhaps it was the alcohol and perhaps I am sick and perhaps Lawrence was right and she will for always be my wife. For another man she can be only his woman. Even if she married she would not be his first wife nor his first love. Pride. Narcissism. What's intrinsically inferior about second?

". . . after a committee meeting."

"I'm sorry. I wasn't listening. You met Robyn. And how is she? And Chris, my little girl, did you see her?"

"My holy God—the noise of these parties and what all. No, I didn't see your little girl. I met Robyn after a SANE committee meeting. The Banners sub-committee. She's fine. She's a lovable person. I know that you don't communicate but she said to look you up."

"Oh."

"I'm Mark. Mark Madden. I'm a bum."

"What sort of a bum?"

"The worst sort—a folk singing bum. I'm afraid I'm not singing for anything tonight. I'm eating and drinking but not singing a note—freeloading."

"You'll sing some other time. Have a drink. Drink is communal. In theory, anyhow."

"Have a drink! That's all you Aussies ever say. These parties! I've got to hand it to you—you fellows can drink."

I watched his face and heard his voice.

"Have you a place to live?"

"No, not as yet."

"Stay with me."

He had a sleeping bag and he slept in that on a settee and I lay in my own double bed. A bed which I was aware was half-empty even when a girl stayed there for a stray hungry night. I wormed naked into the warm zone of the bed and thought of Mark. I had liked his eyes and his voice and his words. Now I thought of his body. And then I wondered about what was happening to me. I put my cheek against a thought which I had never touched. And I slept.

"I feel lost from the world, Sean. I am a wanderer. I am a singer of other people's songs. I walk in other people's lands. I usually sleep in other people's beds. There's no me. There's only other people."

"But what about Oregon and your home?"

"It's ten years since I was there. For God's sake it was never home. It was a man called my father and some woman called my mother. And shit-house brawls. I left as soon as I could walk alone after dark. I was afraid of going but I was afraid to stay. I'm afraid now. But Jesus, we are all afraid."

We looked at our beers and I thought about being afraid. I was more afraid at times when I cared about things and events. I felt afraid now of a *feeling*. And I remembered the things I was afraid of now and then when I cared and I said: "There's a lot to be afraid of. Political things like bombs and being forced to go to war and psychological things like fucked-up sex and being crippled with things like cancer and car accidents. There's neurotic unreality—a thing that can happen to you and you don't realise it until you fall down somewhere and are dragged away screaming."

"You know, Sean, you feel the world the way I feel the world. But I take no risk and no responsibility. At least you take risks—your marriage and your child was a risk—at least you took it. God knows I've never tried. Peace and war. At least you speak on the public platform as a chemist. All I've done was to go to one meeting of the Banners sub-committee—and then only because of some girl. So I sing a few protest songs in some out-of-the-way coffee shops. But that's just by drift—not by decision. Drift and drift. That's me."

"We all drift most of the time. I try now and then, I suppose I try."

There in the alcove of the pub our hands gripped. Mine partly the grip of a mate and partly the grip of a lover. Mark's? How did Mark's hand grip? And then a blush. And then a laugh. And another beer so that we could go normally on. Why did we hold to grim normality?

"MY JESUS! This harbour—and these ferries. They're wild. This mid-morning fog and the city, a ghost over there, grey, and the ships, ghosts, grey. I'm moved by it, Sean."

"People who work on boats are different in the way they work – temperament. They talk to people as if they are people. They're not eroded and suspicious and hostile. These people are refreshed by the sea."

"I believe it."

"Play something."

"I suppose no one would mind. There's hardly anyone on the damn ferry."

The certain strumming. The tuning. The listening ear. The tuning fingers.

"So here's to you, my rambling boy.
May all your rambling bring you joy.
So here's to you my rambling boy."

Some people make you see the world. They make buildings and streets and manhole covers reach out their actuality. The water and the sky touch you. And your footsteps are each important and your breathing.

WE HEARD BEETHOVEN played in the dark as we lay on the carpet and looked through the window at the dark harbour, spotted by moving lights, on a spring night. I wanted to touch him but there is ten miles between two men. And there was Louise he was sleeping with now and then and there was Cindy I said I loved and who I knew would come back to me one day. I cried then. Hoping he'd hear.

"Why do you cry?"

"The music. Wine and my life and its mess and its good times. And for you. And being twenty-nine and the way more dense and confused."

I felt the music joined us and I was touching him through it.

"Why do you cry for me?"

"You mean something to me. You're a close mate." Meaning I feel love for you.

"We're close. We're mates and it's good."

But do you feel love, Mark? You once said I feel the world the way you feel the world. Do you feel me the way I feel you?

"Do you remember Mark, the time we gripped each other's hand?"

"Yes, I do. I remember."

"I was thinking then about that."

I looked to the back of his neck and to his long proud hair and wanted to reach and touch him, but I couldn't.

"I SHOULDN'T but I am."

"Why?"

"Because I'm a restless cunt. I'm a bum. I've always

been restless. I know I won't find peace or whatever it is, if I stay. I can find it only for a time. It has always been like this."

"But we've found a pretty good time."

"But it will go if I stay. I want to go before it goes."

"How do you know it will go?"

"I know. Because all situations destroy themselves. I know."

"Will you come back?"

"Yes. That will be a new situation, then."

"Where will you go?"

"I'll go back through Oregon for God knows what reason. And I'll go to Alaska where I haven't been. Out of this summer into cool snow."

"What do you want, Mark?"

"I don't know. I really don't know. I don't know if I'm searching or avoiding. Kids? A wife who will understand me and bear with my restlessness or dispel it? An end to being restless? Or to be always restless?"

"Play—play something."

He touched the strings. He smiled at me.

"So here's to you, my rambling boy.
May all your rambles bring you joy."

"Remember you played that on the ferry that foggy morning?"

"I remember, Sean, I remember everything we've done."

He sang the song about himself because I couldn't sing it to him. And I felt tight because I could never touch him.

THAT QUAY was blown with wind. It had wheat spilled its splintering length. It has fifteen lights, each not reaching far into the resisting night. At the end of the fifteen lights lay a German tramp steamer with a name I could not pronounce and have not remembered. Mark had his duffle bag and wore his duffle coat. I walked with my hands in my pockets.

"It's a tub."

"It'll probably go no further than the Heads and there sink forever."

"No union rates on this."

No one else was on the dark quay. A long emptiness.

"Well, *bon voyage*, Mark. That's what's to be said, isn't it?"

His hand on my arm. That was allowed.

"They've been sweet months, Sean, sweet, sweet months. Four sweet seasons. I don't know what else can be said."

"That's enough. Four sweet seasons."

The First Story of Nature

ALTHOUGH SHE wanted to become an historian—or, as she sometimes told herself, a serious thinker—she led an impulsive sort of life and was glad that she could. She was glad that there was still *some* of the child in her, that she hadn't frozen into a stiff Apollonian. That would come, she guessed. Her impulse to act would be slowed down and increasingly restrained by questions of whether it would be wise. Had she considered alternatives abcdefghijklmnopqrstuvwxyz? Was she succumbing to the seduction of mood? Didn't she have responsibilities? All these sorts of questions. Or perhaps people never became coldly rational but simply replaced impulse and spontaneity with habit, patterns of living, and styles of life. But rational questions raised their frowning heads at her even now. She could act on impulse, but sometimes, say in the morning while showering or riding the bus to university, she would find herself face-to-face with one of the frowning questions. They frowned like her father. Even thinking like this now after having made an impulsive decision was a sign that the frowning person in her was working against the giggling person—against her decision to live with Hugo. But she had expected it to come. Perhaps all this meant was that she was becoming an intellectual—becoming aware of herself. She would not let it bother her.

"And how old are you?" Hugo had asked, his Nebraskan accent a melody.

"Sweet twenty".

"Do you think age difference is important? I'm exactly sour thirty. Do you think that will bother us? Do you think love is embarrassed by age difference?"

Before she could answer, he went on: "I do not. Love is a rapport fed by an exchange between two people. From you —the insights of youth—from me, the experience (be what it may) of the twenties. Love is a caring and what does age have to do with that? And love is having children and we have bodies that will do that. Where then, may I ask, is the problem?"

Answering his own question with overwhelming definiteness, he said: "There is no problem."

The Nebraskan accent was a Hamelin piper. And his words, too. But that was not the important thing about him and that was not in any way the thing which made her do it. She felt that Hugo seriously wanted a "cohabitating relationship"— strongly and without nonsense. And she wanted it. She felt that she had made adequate allowances for her infatuation with him and that the decision was basically rational. But no, the decision to live with him had been impulsive. The analysis came afterwards and was a summary. What she probably meant was that there was nothing foolish about going to live with Hugo. It offered her things—experience and a close human relationship etc.

When he had turned to her during the film and said "For God's sake, Cindy— let's live together," she had replied, without thought or resistance, "Yes."

"We don't know much about each other," she had said, meaning it not as hesitation, but as a way of saying "Isn't it wonderful that not knowing each other doesn't matter— we have rapport." She told herself that "knowing" people wasn't a test in which a certain number of correct answers had to be given.

She hesitated before the word, she feared it had an

avalanche of implications. ". . . love . . . I guess, is rapport," she said to him.

He said they would have a lifetime to find out about each other. "Even then we will not know everything."

She was determined to be certain about this. Certainty was lacking in everything else. But she accepted this. Uncertainty she supposed, was a natural state for anyone who thought. But in a human relationship one could find certainty.

"ARE WE HAVING only potatoes?" she asked. He was cooking the meals until she had become "acclimatized" (as Hugo put it) to him and his house.

"Yes. With lemon juice—baked potatoes with lemon—with butter—with pepper and salt. Delightful." He spoke with exuberance.

She hid a hungry disappointment.

He continued, like a salesman: "Simple, wholesome potatoes. I like simple wholesome cooking. I've done a list of my favourite dishes. Of course, you'll have yours, too. I argue that there is too much confusion of flavour and too much spicing in modern cooking. I like the meals of the pioneers and peasants."

She watched him serve, caught helpless by a new situation. Her disappointment went. A bowl of baked potatoes—a beautiful dark wooden bowl—two wooden platters—a pile of coarse black bread—two sliced lemons, yellow—and deep yellow North Coast butter. He made a side salad.

Her eyes liked it. And her mouth, she ate the potatoes and found their taste for the first time. She was able to savour them. After, they ate mixed, unsalted nuts.

Hugo was "primitive" in other ways. He ground his own pepper, coffee, herbs, flour, and baked a type of bread, and extracted fruit and vegetable juices by a special process, and ate only unrefined sugar.

As a chemist he knew about the properties of food. "I will teach you the real arts of cooking," he laughed. "How to really use food. Do you know why our teeth rot out, our hair falls out, why we get ulcers and cancer? It's because of our over-refined diet. Old Henry Miller had a delightful essay on it. I'll hunt it out for you."

"My parents' teeth haven't fallen out."

"They will—or perhaps they escaped as children."

He said that modern food manufacturing was criminal.

He must have partially indoctrinated her because she felt guilty when she threw away the raisin sandwiches she'd made for lunch—at Hugo's direction. She ate two meat pies instead. The guilt came from feeling that she was betraying Hugo—or betraying herself by not being able to openly resist. Then the guilt dissolved to resentment. She did not follow the resentment because it led down an overgrown track. She laughed it off saying, "You're becoming *so* self-analytical."

Usually she did not mind the natural cooking which Hugo taught her. Now and then she cooked him grilled steak with onions, chips, eggs and fried tomatoes and he complained about the fats or she cooked him something from *Cooking Greek Style* and he joked that she was killing him with spices.

Hugo and she fished in the harbour and he talked of hunting and fishing trips in the Nebraskan forests and once in Canada, before he'd fled the USA as a "nuclear refugee."

"We'll go hunting one day and in the evening you can cook the food we've hunted and then you will really come to know the natural life."

"I've always had a repugnance for hunting, for killing animals."

"You'll get over that. It's OK if the food hunted is eaten. For sport—no. But hunting is at the very heart of natural existence."

SHE HAD HURT a boy to come impulsively to live with Hugo. Bobby had been seeing her at lectures during the first year and taking her to film screenings, buying her coffee in the foyer, and having lunch with her on the grass. Nothing about love had been spoken, but in the second year she had bought her first pills and after a few timid circlings they had slept together—clutching each other and trembling—his elbow pinning her hair to the pillow—both sweating with tension. Still, it was good. It was exploratory for them both and she accepted it as that. She was relieved also that the "first time" was behind her. Perhaps this had been a big part of the satisfaction. She remembered little else.

She had not told Bobby about Hugo at first although it happened so quickly and there was so little to tell. Over coffee in the foyer she had told him she was leaving Betty and Jill's flat to live with Hugo. Bobby had been upset and told her that she was being stupid, had stood up and abruptly said that he had to go.

She had shrugged and said that there had been nothing between them really, she hadn't pledged herself. She felt irritated by unreasonable guilt.

Hugo's way of life was a second crossroad taking her in yet another direction, and taking her further from her suburban upbringing. She had moved a long distance from baked Sunday dinners, cold meat and salad in the summer, and Chinese food in saucepans from the Dragon Restaurant on the corner, once a week. She was not of the suburbs anymore. She had known that when she left home to live with Betty and Jill, when she stopped reading *Women's Weekly* and found her way, lost and unguided, in Betty's *New Yorkers*. She was not dramatically *alienated* but she was bound in her own direction. She was glad that she could expose herself to Hugo and that she had flexibility to go in a way that was different.

Yet there was the resentment and the confusion which was the overgrown track. Without vanity, she saw herself as an intelligent, independent, and unneurotic girl (certainly not as neurotic as Betty—or Jill). Yet some of her reactions to Hugo were uncontrollable and they battered her—as though he was holding her fists and hitting her with them. She kept her reactions secretly held down because they were foolish. The reactions were mainly from housework and cooking and his attitudes to them.

She had been doing the housework while he was out, as she preferred to. He had returned early.

Kissing her he said, "It warms me to see you cleaning the cave."

She gagged an outcry which rose in her.

"Hygiene is essential for survival," she said standing behind her mock rationality. "I was just finishing up." And she put away the cleaner leaving the work uncompleted. Two hours later she recognised that she had felt degraded by him. By him seeing her doing the work and by his remarks.

They were drinking beer from his twenty-ounce Mexican pewters. It was the time for what Hugo called called "looking over the day."

"I think we should share cleaning the house," she said, aggressively.

He drank a large mouthful. "I agree, I agree," he said, and then, pointedly, "we do."

He in fact did more than she, but she disputed peevishly and on a technicality. The toilet.

"I know. I want a clean toilet. I think it is important and I appreciate the work you put in on it," he said. "I simply cannot come at it—it bugs me. I have a thing about toilets." He gave a big shrug.

She had a thing about toilets too but did not let it into the conversation. It was opposite to his. He had an aversion to cleaning them: she had a compulsion. Tiredly, she acknowledged that her mother did too.

He gave her, from time to time, kitchen efficiency lessons. When he did she switched off into a hostile buzz. She couldn't receive them and usually didn't apply them. He seemed to know more about the kitchen than she did.

"I come from a family of boys," he said, laughing at her sarcastic query, "and I lived as a bachelor for three years. Two training schools."

So he tended to cook and clean more frequently and better than she. She read during it, closed-down by her weird tension, seeing the print and not the words. When she did cook she slopped and burnt and when she cleaned she did so secretively and without patience.

Hugo's comment about *him* hunting and *her* cooking returned to her often. She would have an angry inner dialogue. She was not a squaw. Yet when he had said it she had felt a warm emotional touch and had roughly and intellectually pushed it away. She was going to be an academic, not just a woman—and never a squaw. She was a woman biologically—because she had a vagina. But she did not feel "womanly" whatever that was. She was not going to be socially conditioned to some *Women's Weekly* idea of woman. She was going to be an intellectual with a vagina—like de Beauvoir. She was not going to be like other poor, deluded things. She could not analyse the stupid conflicts about housework but saw them as examples of how woman was moulded by her society if she didn't fight it. How they were socially conditioned to want to be servile and to do petty menial tasks. But she became tired of chasing these sorts of conflicts and tried to ignore them as best she could.

Then came the remark.

Hugo liked her for her simplicity.

"I like your simple clothes and I like your graceful ways. I know precisely how you will dress our children and how they'll imitate their mother's grace."

The remark reminded her. "Talking of children, have you seen my orals? I left them on the ledge in the bathroom but they're not there."

He looked at her solemnly. With hard Nebraskan authority he said, "I threw them away." And then smiled directly and warmly at her.

She was amazed. Struck.

"You what?"

He turned the book he was reading face down on the table.

"I threw them away. They outraged me."

She shook her head.

"I hate contraceptives," he said. "I hate to think of your

body being twisted by chemicals."

She was having difficulty composing a sentence. She said something like: "What!"

"I want children," he said loudly, gesticulating the expression "So-what-the-hell-is-wrong-with-that?"

"You must be out of your mind," she said.

"Love goes bad between people when they don't want children," he said. "Contraception is a rejection. A rejection of me as a father. It's hesitancy." He talked quickly.

She remained standing at the bathroom door, toothbrush in her hand.

"But—I've got a year to go at uni—we've never even discussed it. It's unbelievable." She was rigid with anger.

"Love implies children," he said, buttressing his words with a heavy definiteness. "Children are the other part of the natural equation."

"What crap. What crap. What shit."

"No. It's true."

"I don't give a damn about children. You threw away my pills. You authoritarian shit."

She remembered other things he'd done. Theatre bookings without her consultation. Things like that.

"You didn't ask me whether you could use them. You didn't tell me you were using them. Who imposed on who?" he shouted.

"For God's sake only a fool wouldn't—you're—you're like all men—you think we can be used for your—fantasies."

He didn't move his hands from the table where they lay palms down in front of him. As though he was about to rise. He began to colour.

"So children are a fantasy. You're hung up—hung up on modern crap about independence. You think being independent means being neuter—you're hung up, Cindy."

"You monster."

"Having children means being a woman. That would scare the living shit out of you."

"I don't want to be a woman," she yelled, sensing the

bad tactics of the admission. "I mean I don't want to be that sort of woman. Your sort of shithouse, servile woman."

He seemed to collapse in a hopeless way.

"You're sick," she yelled.

He raised his hands in a gesture of futility. He stood up. He reached out to her with his hands. His eyes followed hopelessly behind. He tried to take her in his arms. She pulled away and went to the bedroom. She heard him break down. Cold and frightened she piled some of her things into her wicker basket. *He had tried to force children on to her.* In the kitchen he was sobbing at the sink with his back to her. She left the house, saying: "I'm going." *It was male domination.* And she was humiliated by the demoralising power of the things he had said. But they were crazy things. *His attitude was authoritarian. He resented the independence that the pill gave her.* She wouldn't become involved again—she would have lovers— but not the involvement of domesticity. *One didn't have to have children.* In a mental skip she was nauseated by the thought of the sexual act. Instantly she was embarrassed by guilt and severely expurgated the nausea from her mind. She gathered her principles and theories around her like bedclothes. She almost ran down the street in emotional panic. Wondering where to go and wondering about the mess of it. "I had no alternative," she said, and she herself heard how positive and how desperate it sounded and the sound frightened her. Oh shit, Oh christ.

SICKNESS

Nish's Sour Desire

AND WALKING NOW chief-clerkily, along that people- and vehicle-stewing street, conscious even then of the office key standing in his pocket. The key which seemed, now and then, to give more pride-pleasure to him than any erection he'd had for so long. Sitting there it wore away the twice-repaired, key-chair-and-desk worn grey suit that remained bent at the elbow when hung and which covered, as he walked, his loose, wash-grey, sagging underwear which covered his loose, grey, sagging body.

Then seeing her.

Her desirability more strong than the twenty or so desirable images that forever disturbed his drowsy day. The images of the long-haired, bouffant-haired, prominently-breasted, pushed-out-bellied females that disturbed his drowsy day. The images that made him wriggle and finger his desire and then chase it away because of the sickness that came to him as his wife again squatted on his mind.

The girl in the street waiting. For the bus? He walking slower now for the longer looking that it gave him. Those prominent breasts. Oh, for the supple youngness. Wasn't it true that despite balding, dandruff, bellying, and screwed up eyes and forehead, young girls wanted middle-aged men? Not always for their money but sometimes for their utter, genial, male maturity? Wasn't it true? Wasn't it in *Truth* now and then, to disturb him and make him wriggle and finger his desire on warm Sundays in the lounge chair when involved with the disappointing excitement and remote pleasure of other people's fulfilment detailed in the three Sunday papers. If only one could climb in through the printing, away from Sunday morning. Away from cups of tea from an over-stained, never-washed, teapot poured by a teapot wife.

And didn't he carry the key of the door of the office as chief clerk? Did that mean nothing? There was a time too when he had been a very good swimmer. With some promise. Could there just be that one chance that one girl so young and so desirably supple and sexual could be attracted to him? Even if he had only key-dignity. But he could be witty. Pull in the stomach. Perhaps with a little exercise. Somewhere at home there was a plan for making money. But surely it could happen, and must happen to him because he was not destined to a lifelong of dull, panting, sexual friction with his wife, and those negative, sometimes disturbed days at the office with visits to the toilet twice a day in office time. How fierce he spat his slime against the toilet wall every day. Didn't he always feel that he was meant for different and it would be soon? He had seen erotic escape to other worlds only glimpsed in the printing of *Truth* and when on the dreaming toilet. Couldn't this girl at this bus stop be the girl strayed from his erotic, printed pastures, now waiting to lead him to it?

Isn't she now eyeing him and isn't there an asking twitch about her lipstick lips? Oh, let it be yes. If it be yes then never again would he go to the office and its toilet and its corrections from the accountant. Let this be yes and it would be away to other places, in through the printing never again to sleep next to his plumbing-stomached wife. If this girl was his he could stride across the world.

He would approach her. He would break the glass windows which separate each man and each woman walking in city streets. Windows that allow each to see and watch each other but never to talk or hear. Shaking cold with his courage, knowing that this was the impulse of greatness, stopping then before her at the bus stop and speaking. And she replying. But her quick-smiling reply falling like sudden rain. Her reply being her price which had not appeared in her advertisement.

Going with her. Though dull and dazed by misjudgement. Led by his penis. But . . . but wasn't there a possibility that she would go away with him when he offered her pastures? Wouldn't she also be looking for a chance of away? Like him. Oh, wasn't she more likely because she had no surroundings which clawed her when she wanted to move? Not like the women of the suburbs. She would be a woman without the lead of staying heavy inside her. Hadn't he read somewhere? And wasn't this then a chance? He would tell her before he finished, while on top, because he knew that when he finished everything seemed sour and tired.

And her arse tight and firm beneath her supple hips, and he inside, choking and wringing with his hope.

Nish

TRUDGING UP the narrow stairway, rolling and over-salivating his cigarette, away from the accountant's office and to the toilet, and on the toilet seat making a spit in his mouth, moulding it and then driving it out against the wall. Watching it slide and hearing again the gratifying words . . .

"Come in, Mr Nish," the accountant had said, looking up from his skinny writing. "Come in. It's the William's policy—can't find a record of it. Says he's been paying in for twenty years."

And with his stains and chief-clerkly tone of concern he had sat half-way forward on the chair with his feet overlapped and said: "No record?"

"No record at all," the accountant said, rolling his pencil between his fingers.

"That's very odd."

"Very odd indeed."

"Records don't disappear."

"No, one wouldn't think so."

And now sitting in the serenity of the toilet, his only solitude in the nightly-daily somersault of his crowded-train routine. He so hated those public toilets with inspection windows. The toilet being serenity and safety from his agitated accountant, his twittering office girls, his teapot wife, and his stuff-nosed sons. Everyone always wanting him and pestering. Coming in on him and making him hastily fold up his thinking and his dreams for fear they would be seen. But then knowing to himself that they couldn't and smiling to himself without showing it and giggling with himself without noise.

AND NOW, coming home from a prostitute, out of the dark, urine-and-Solyptol flavoured lanes into the bright, laminex and detergent kitchen preferring the smells of human escapade from the prostitution-lanes. Lying beside his fat-disfigured, lumpy-legged wife, and thinking thoughts sexually grotesque and at the same time talking about the garden to her. Going into his wife, without having washed, and soon coming. The lingering shape and salacious stance of the prostitute giving him his erection. Never her. Once with a prostitute is never enough. Giggling without noise. And she thinking that she did right by opening her legs and lying back with eyes closed and breath clutched waiting for him to finish so that she could make a cup of tea and have a Bex before bed. Thinking then about his spittings on the office toilet wall. There were browny stains on the wall from him and he knew that no one knew who did it. Lying there prodding his other delectably secret mental thing. The secret of his secrets. His defiance, his spit, against the accountant, against paper insurance, against smothering tons of filing, but most against his lumpy wife—he being not insured. Holding the fact tight in his mind's hands. His secret of his secrets. And she all the time thinking of the lump sum of money she would get when he died and became a lump in the ground. Smiling now without showing it and giggling without noise.

NOW DOWN at the Apex Club flicking through his secrets, standing there among the suits and ties and badges. Seeing his secrets as glossy, dirty pictures. Running through them like Catholic beads—dark-street prostitution, toilet-writing masturbation, evil-dreaming, toilet-spitting, and record-burning. Shaking hands with the honoured guest speaker and being introduced as Mr Nish, chief clerk. Trying to turn over all his secret pictures fast so that they became one almost unbearably delectable impression. And saying fast to himself—Mr Nish, chief fucker, chief puller, chief spitter, and chief burner, as he genially shook the guest speaker's hand.

AND NOW BEING HOT and watching the typist's thighs, shown by her pulled-up skirt, not pulled up just far enough for him to see, even when she flapped it for coolness. The rocket of his desire spluttering. He taking the records of a Mrs Turner in his hand, bitten with the idea of erasing Mrs Turner from the world of insurance, and feeling that year by year he could erase everyone from world until the typist and her hot, sun-browned thighs were left for him. Collecting the policy, every form and card with Mrs Turner's name and burning them in a hole near the pumpkins at the back of his yard. And then his third destruction coming after seeing a girl leaning on a filing cabinet squashing her breasts against it. Thinking to himself how aware she was of the feeling of her breasts against the hard metal. The glimpse burning him and he burning another set of records in the hole. And knowing that no one knew where the files went or why, made him vibrant.

So much of his living being hot, uncomfortable, sometimes slumberous, sitting around, now and then disturbed by splutters of pleasant itchiness, and now and then burning with rockets of frustrations, and now and then tinged and sweetened by secret defilements. No one knowing who left the brown spit marks on the wall of the world and he seeing the day coming when all his life would be secret and hidden and he would be alone, serene, in a toilet world.

Dry Munching

HIS FEELINGS SWAM in murky alcohol towards the idea of loving her which had to come first before the idea of entering her could respectably come. She in her loneliness and shame and suffering would cling to him although he was called as a boy "the professor" and laughed at for his feet.

As was usual, he drank with Cobbie, the blind weaver with the pin head.

He did not want to enter her but love her and yet he did not want to love her but enter her and have her love him. He then rose in righteousness and whipped away thoughts of entering her body. And his mind panted with the whipping.

The squeaking voice of Cobbie said: "You're preoccupied to-night, Samuel. I divine big love problems."

How did squeaking Cobbie know, who had never been loved except by his mother and then not truly?

"Love problems probleming love problems, Cobbie my lad."

"More then of the fluid of contentment, Samuel my lad."

"Yes, Cobbie my lad, more then of that."

He munched his thoughts, moving his jaws cuddishly and blinking his eyes like small irritated shutters.

Frog-mouthed, he drank his beer down in frog-gulps.

"Must be away then, Cobbie, for the hour—no longer, my lad. Stay watch on the hotel. Do not move."

Splay-footed, he paved his way towards the hospital.

She was broken with shame no doubt and in dread that the world would despise her for her fall and fatherless child. But he would go now to her with heart gifts and would munch his thoughts of love and blink down at her and be gentle although she was fallen and dirty and spoiled. He would raise her to goodness. He would possess her entirely and she would devote herself to him. He alone in the world would want her.

He bought then a magazine and chocolates and flowers and books and oranges from railway station stalls. On the train to the maternity hospital he wrote on page twenty-seven of the magazines: "Anne is your name and you are my love. I will take you away and you will be my wife." He wrote with biro and thought of writing in a stronger, more personal fluid. But he rose up and told himself: "Expunge those thoughts from your mind, Samuel, and be pure. You come to take this girl from the depths of her sin." And he sat and munched and nodded his head to the train and the outside night.

"Old waddle" is what the boys yelled at him when he walked from the school as a boy, smelling of bananas and camphor. He had waddled ever since through the bars and brothels of the city never yet having drunk enough so that no more was needed the next day nor entered enough women so that another was not needed the next night. Oh, he wanted the drink that satiated and the sex that calmed.

He had noticed the poor, fallen, pregnant girl with beatnik clothes, laughing to hide her shame and drinking in despair. He had watched her with compassion. He knew compassion because he felt it for himself. He was not tricked by her laughing and the flippant people who surrounded her. She had no real friends but him and he owned her happiness. He saw her sad heart because he saw his own and he knew the sadness of the world. And now she was not drinking or laughing but in hospital to climax her shame. He would come to her. The others would not care and would drink and would forget her.

She, he, and Cobbie, the blind weaver, would live in one large, cool house away from the jeering and the ignorant and they would never go back to the hotel or see others.

Cool hospital wards. His heart ran ahead of him, like a mangy dog, across the clean-polished ward floor.

She was alone and sadly lying.

"My name is Samuel and you are Anne. I bring you gifts and something to read."

He could see that she was puzzled with joy.

"Why, thank you, Samuel."

He stood munching thoughts of love and blinking them down on her with gentle forgiveness and looking at her breasts so large and out-pushing.

He did not speak because he was saying in another language. He stood and munched and waited for her to say: "Yes, I'll come away with you." She wriggled in the bed as his thoughts penetrated her.

His parcels loaded the bed.

He would wait.

Then she said: "Won't you sit down? You're from the hotel aren't you? I thought I knew your face."

"I am Samuel."

Then there was a quake. A young man rocked the ward. He wore jeans and had hair that reached his shirt. Who was he and how did he dare to come? He took the girl's hand and kissed her. Who was he to do such a thing? He watched in a munching daze. This man was not wanted! He would drag the man out from the hospital and to the gutter! He moved his feet. "Old Waddle" they called him once. Then the quake stopped.

"I'd like you to meet Anderson Fith," she said.

But with three words of his mother's politeness he took his leave and waddled away. The man had made him hot and wet and sick. He had left behind the magazine with the message in it and it would be read and laughed at by the fallen girl and the evil man. He thought he heard them laugh as he waddled away. He thought he heard them yell, "Old Waddle!" Let them.

And in the pub he went to Cobbie who squeaked: "Job complete? Ready for the business of the evening, Samuel my lad?"

His feelings simmered, but not away, as he drank down beer with Cobbie. A word moved between them now and then. Cobbie looking nowhere with no eyes, he blinking nowhere with clouded eyes, knowing once again that the world was hateful and one must be wary lest the world deceived you into meddling with its dirt. One must ever be above the world, nodding and munching, alone.

Bread, Sugar, and Milk

"MOTHER DARLING. I'm feeling bloody awful. Positively awful. I want you to ring work—yes sweetheart—no, that's all right."

What does the old bitch care?—wrapped up in the parcel of her own petty ailments. Self-centred old age.

"I don't know, Mother. Pains everywhere. In every bloody muscle. Tell them flu. Why do I swear? I feel like swearing, that's why I'm swearing, Mother. Yes, and in the head, too. That's precisely what I intend to do, I'm going straight to bed now. You shan't forget to ring the office. You know I can't face him. Thank you, darling. Bye."

Phone.

Table.

Carpet.

Wall.

Flat. Sick in a sick flat. Bernie always saying: "It's so tasteful, Donnie." As tasteful as a fart. Nothing in my bloody queeny life is tasteful.

Remember those sweet days forty years ago? Liar. Dear Donnie, it's forty-five years since you were a little child and you smelt and felt the sweet smell and the unbearable mystery of mother's underwear—how the sheen of silk felt like the supple skin of the warm deep parts of mother, and how you took the underwear from her drawer and put it in the cot with you and how they found it in the cot with you and how they found it and took it away, puzzled. What must they have thought?

The house was polished, quiet, clean and mother loved me then. Who loves me now? Not Bernard. I remember how, as a child, I was sick and she put me in the guest's room away from Jerry and I stared my way into the pictures on the wall, along the foreign roads in them. And after a hot bath, dried by mother on a cold tiled floor, I would wriggle down into the cool folded-back sheets, freshly laundered and smelling of fresh air, wrung by the hands of mother.

And oh Jesus I am sick now. Fill the hot water bottle. She gave me lemonade and presents when I was ill. Who cares for me now when I am sick? No one. Where is the lemonade and bananas and ice cream? Why must I live in loneliness without Mother, without anyone? Who cares if I die? Who? Tell me who? At forty-eight.

Enough bloody drama. Get into bed you old fool—you're heading towards the psychiatric clinic. If Bernard was here I'd make him look after me. Why did he go away on holidays without me? The bastard! The unfeeling bastard. So he's crazy about Mervyn. He could still spare me *some feeling*. Aspirin, what the hell, they do no bloody good. Remember how when you were sick as a child Mother gave you bread and milk and sugar—hot milk. Bread and hot milk and sugar. It was sweet and warm and Mother would feed it to me spoonful by spoonful as she sat on the bed near me and I could smell her underwear. Oh, Mother, mother, why do you leave me here alone? Let me come back. Let me come back to your lap and to the sweet milky days. Let me.

You're going off your head, you neurotic old fool. But make some. It was good for me then when I was sick, it will be good for me now. Eating my childhood. Put in the milk—mustn't boil. Cut the bread into slices. Cut off the crusts. Put into bowl. Must have hot bath first. Turn off milk until after.

Remember how you would pull yourself in the bath? God bless mummy and God bless daddy. Wasn't the hot so very, very hot and wasn't the cold so cold? Remember Mother asking why I was so long in the bath? Remember soaping yourself up to erection with Mother's scented soap? And loving the scent—and then scrubbing it off for fear that the boys at school would smell you and tease you? But some always stayed faintly and you smelled it secretly during the day with quiet, dear excitement. Remember looking through the bathroom cabinet and wondering what the stuff in the bottles was for and wondering if any had anything to do with sex? But you weren't a baby then.

Lorna's baby. Smelly, detestable thing. Vomiting and shitting. Why did she hand it to me? I told her I would drop it. Why did she give the smelling thing to me? She knew I'd drop it. I told her I'd drop it. Why then did she give it to me? I dropped it and she was to blame. The silly bitch with her clammy baby. Detestable babies. Watch out for your cigarette, she yelled. The silly bitch. I could have stubbed it in the baby's eye for all I care. I told her I would drop it so why did she give it to me? I told her I would burn it. But she said: "Nurse the baby, Uncle Donald. Have a nurse of Sara. Have a nurse of her, go on." I told her I would drop it and she said watch out for the cigarette or I'd burn the baby and I would burn it, too—the dirty little baby will grow into a haughty bitch with a rough, rasping cunt. I told her I would drop it, she's to blame for giving it to me.

Dry now with a big woolly towel. Why isn't anyone here to dry me? I'm too sick. Put on my flannel pyjamas buttoned up at the neck. Oh shit, I am sick—the pain of it. I'm ill, ill, ill—but bread, sugar and milk will make me feel better. Little again, safe again. Hot water bottle in bed. Milk's ready. Pour over the bread and sugar. Mother, Mother, come to me and feed me. Mother, make my bed soon, for I'm sick at the heart and fain would lie down. Eat it in bed. Prop yourself up with pillows.

"There you are, dearest, now eat this and you'll feel better. Poor little Donniekins is sick. Eat this my duddies." The soft body to snuggle against as she sits down on my bed, breasts to snuggle to. "Eat your bread and milk, dearest one." For these are sweet milky days.

"Will I be in bed long, Mother?"

"No not long, duddy—not long now. You'll soon be well again and going out to play. Eat up."

"Where's Daddy?"

"Daddy's out."

"I'm glad there's just you and me."

"Are you darling? Eat your bread and milk. So am I glad."

"Will it make me better?"

"Yes, it will make you better, eat it all up."

No. No. No. No. Oh, shit. Oh, shit, no.

Gagging.

Tears.

Wretchedness.

Retch.

Retch.

Retchedness.

Now I've spewed on the bed. That's all I bloody needed. What a bloody mess. All over the cover. Vile. How putrid. What's happening to me? I'm going mad. Why? Cry, go on, cry. It used to taste so beautiful. And it's good for sick people. Good things turn bad. The world is a miserable cheat. It cheats me even when I'm sick. Pieces of bread like turds in white piss. Why was everything so good when I was little and now so foul? It's a foul life. Life is foul.

Who wants to be forty-eight? No one gives a bugger about you when you are forty-eight. Miserable old fool. Go on, cry, you old fool. Feel sorry for yourself. Pull the cover off and put it on the floor. Mess. Cry, cry, cry. Take three nembutals and sleep it off. Take the lot why don't you? You never have the guts and it's what you want to do.

Thank God for nembutal. At least they are always there if it ever becomes unbearable. After tomorrow there is work. If only I could stay asleep. If only I could stay drunk —asleep or drunk. But oh why did bread, sugar and milk have to be a cheat? Why couldn't I have it the way it used to be? Why is the world cruel? Why must good things turn bad? Why can't I eat my childhood without being cheated. Mother, why?

I *Am a Very* Clean *Person*

AND STEPPING FROM the bath she spread bath bubbles smelling of chemical violets and patted her body with powder smelling of allure. Both smells squabbled with the rose from her soap and the powder fell around her both on to the cold yellow tiles and on to any fresh air uncaptured by the hot-water steam and the bath smells. Her body was prodded by bones and her breasts hung small and droopy like double chins. Her public hairs were a tangle cringing from the scent and from the powder—clutching their tang. Her flesh held back from her skin because of its sweetness. The chemical lemon made her hair a stranger. The spray deodorant made her armpits shrink and her arse-crack clutch itself tight. And she made her cunt pharmaceutical with a vaginal cream.

THEN THERE WAS a fight because he was too rough with her in bed. Rough with his hands and knees. As though he was clawing at her. Why couldn't he just get done with it?

You're a shit, Doug.

You're a double shit.

You're a king shit and I was happier when I was here on me own.

You can stay here on your own for all I care. See if anyone else wants to fuck you.

Don't talk to me like that.

I'll talk to you any bloody way I want to.

And she tried to push him from the bed but he was too big. And they lay there then in the hot, angry air of the bed.

IT WAS HER FLAT and she had made it the way it was before him. It was her TV and her chiming clock and her carpets and her standard lamp and her bedspread and her maple china cabinet and her maple radiogram. It was all hers. And the flat was clean and spick and span because of her. He was the one who made the mess in it. Not her. And he made a mess in her and on the sheets. She didn't know whether it worse to have it in her or on the sheets. The only pleasure in sex for her was when it was over and she could douche with warm water and Solyptol. Sex was men's pleasure. After he was finished she had to get up out of bed with a Kleenex held against her cunt to stop it running out and have a douche. He just lay there on his back panting and sweating on the sheets. Men were disgusting. And he was rough with his fingers in bed. He could never be gentle. Not him. She only felt right again after the douche. Why weren't men as clean as women?

THE GIRLS AT WORK think I'm thirty-one and still a virgin. They think I'm plain and can't get men. But I got Doug and I sleep with him. I got him at Shirley's New Year's Eve party. He was shy because he has one leg shorter than the other but I don't care. He's still a man. He can be a shit but so can all men. All they are good for is making a mess around the place. And I was married once, when I was seventeen, but he shot through. The girls at the office don't know that. That's one thing they don't know. They can have their giggles but I do as good a job as they do and I have my secrets. They're not a bad bunch. But I have my secrets that they can't get.

I am a very clean person. I have my own towel and soap and washer and toothbrush and toothpaste at work and another lot at home. I have no ugly body odours and my mouth stays fresh all day. I may not be beautiful but I think being clean is more important. Every Friday I wax my desk and polish it so that it smells nice and clean when I come in on Mondays. None of the other girls do that.

I don't know how some people can bear to be as filthy as they are. Men are dirty by nature. Doug is no exception. But he does wash the car. Sometimes after he's hurt me he feels sorry and washes the car, which is something. But it doesn't stop the bruises. He's a beast sometimes but so are all men. I'd like to know how many times I've said "Stop it Dougie you're hurting me."

I like the smell of:
fly spray
antiseptic
floor polish
window cleaner

dry cleaning
Murlex
cold enamel
sunburn cream
But I don't like the smell of:
cum
fat
toilets
sweating
grease
hair
musty rooms
candles
meat

My flat is too small and I sit at home after tidying up and have nothing to do except watch TV and nobody wants to watch TV all the time. Not having enough to do is no good for anyone.

Dougie, why don't we get a bigger flat?

What for?

Because it would be nicer.

We got plenty of room here.

But it would be nice.

It'd cost more money.

What do you mean, more money? I pay the bloody rent, not you. You've got a hide talking about money. All you ever do with money is put it in the machines at the club.

I want to pay but you won't let me.

I wouldn't take money from you because then you'd start bossing me around and telling me what to do. No fear. I know your form. Men are all the same.

Get fucked.

You get fucked.

You shit.

You double shit.

You king shit.

Get out.

I won't get out.

Get out. This is my flat. Get out. You give me the shits.

I won't get out. No woman is going to tell me to get out.

Then he knocked over the vase I got for my twenty-first and spilled the water on the carpet and broke the vase and mucked up the hydrangea that were in it.

You shit. Now look what you've done. Always making a mess. And the vase is broken and I got it for my twenty-first.

You did it.

I didn't do it.

You pushed.

You broke it.

Why don't you drop dead?

Why don't you?

Why don't you get fucked?

Why don't you get out? You make me sick.

You're not going to tell me what to do.

Go to the pub or somewhere where you belong.

I'm staying.

You're an animal.

You're a bitch.

I WENT TO Mr Turner the landlord about a bigger flat. Fuck Dougie. If he doesn't want to move, bugger him. I was a lot better off when I was on my own. I want a change in my life. Everyone is entitled to a change. Dougie says the flat I want is too big. He says that it will cost too much but I've worked it out and I'll be able to manage. I don't know what it's got to do with him anyway. I don't like little flats. You can do things with a big flat.

The new flat has eight windows, a glass front door where I can have a wrought-iron fly-screen door put on. And it has two bedrooms, one where Dougie can sleep when he comes home drunk from the club. He can sleep there instead of snoring all night and keeping me awake and groping at me and making a mess over the sheets or in me. He never knows where he is half the time, when he's drunk. He always wants sex when he's drunk. I can't stand the smell of beer on men. And I can lock the door of my room and keep him out whenever I feel like it. It has a big dining-room and a sun room. I'll have plenty to do. I will get a new vacuum. The sun comes in the sun room so I'll have to put up venetians so that the carpet won't fade.

Housework takes me away from things. I get into a sort of trance when I do it. I like getting rid of all the dirt and grease. The feeling I get from cleaning a greasy stove and seeing it come up clean and bright is a funny feeling. It's a real nice feeling. It makes me hot. I like the way Ajax smells and the way it eats into the dirt. And then I can touch the parts of the stove and they aren't greasy or slimy but hard and shining and smooth and clean. I like the exercise from cleaning. I like a place clean so that you can put your fingers anywhere and not feel any slime or grease. I don't like children because they are always snotty and greasy and they leave greasy marks on everything. I like clean windows that are hard and glassy and you can touch them with your hands and not get dirty marks. I like wooden floors and the smell of polish. I like stainless steel sinks because you can clean them and they are cool and hard and dry with those shining ridges. I like to run my fingers over them. The hard ridges of clean smooth steel. It makes me feel good inside.

I like to see little lumps of greasy fat disappear as I rub. I like to see muck come out of cracks when I clean them with a nail. I like to scrape around plug-holes and get all the muck and dirt out, down the hole as far as I can get. I like to see those brown shitty stains on toilets go away and I scrub with the big loop brush right down in the bowl and up where you can't see. Dougie splashes everywhere when he's had a few drinks. Dougie leaves a mess wherever he goes. He leaves a pissy mess of beer and drops cigarette butts into the bowl. All I seem to do is go around after him cleaning up his mess. Men's messes. Like some sort of slave. The dirt can never touch me because I wear rubber gloves. And that makes me feel good too. To put my hand in dirty places and not get dirty.

I can't stand him around when I'm cleaning. I like to be

on my own. He hates me when I'm cleaning. I sing and hum when I clean and I perspire and feel different. Then I love to sit down afterwards and just relax and feel good inside. I can feel it down my legs and arms—all over. As though I've done something and something has happened to me.

One day I would like to own my own house. I would like there to be no men. But if there were no men there would only be dust. I don't like dry dusty cleaning as much as greasy, mucky cleaning. It's funny but it's true. I like things to be dry and clean when I'm finished but not at first. At first I like them to be greasy as long as I don't have to touch them with my hands.

Will Power + Natural Sex-Drive + Intelligence + Personal Organisation + Aggression = Sexual Success

HIS MOTHER WAS a cultured person with fine sensibilities. She was delicate, intelligent and now, old. But these were conventional things to say about one's mother. She was something more. The word he thought was "noble." She was a noble woman. But this wasn't the reason, or at least not the main reason, why he had to stop masturbating. He had to stop for any number of reasons. His age, for instance: thirty-three. His only notable failure in life so far was the absence of a wife and family—if that could be called failure, and he supposed it could. His mother never commented now about that. He supposed that it would be a cruel thing to talk about at his age. At thirty-three. There were things one joked about at twenty-eight which would be insensitive to mention at thirty-three. But there were the other main reasons why he should stop. There was the central fact that it *diverted* his drive from women. That was what had caused him to be so inactive about women. He had picked up the blessed Habit at twelve—was it at twelve? He remembered clearly the guilty ecstasy which had come so surprisingly from the inexplicable urge he had to fondle himself. But it was this Habit which had diverted him for so long. He had, for instance, been in love with Donna, he was almost sure of that, but because of the Habit his natural drive had waned and gone away in the sheets of his bed instead of spurring him on to her and to between her legs. He could see it all now. He was bloody good at retrospect. History training, training in being wise after the event. It was his history training which was his greatest weakness. Always interested —over-interested—in the past. Always insufficiently interested in the present. Donna had been a very sweet person and he had respected her thoroughly. They had never gone to bed but then, she was not that type of woman. He remembered, though, a kiss outside the faculty office one night after a reception.

A full kiss—almost orgasmic. He had controlled himself or God knows what would have happened. He had doused his sexual thoughts. He had feared that if he displayed his real feelings she would have run a mile. But looking back perhaps he was wrong and perhaps he should have been more . . . aggressive. Take the way he was polishing his glasses now. It was all so . . . passive—and introspective. Like an old woman. Like in very fact, his mother. But that was too simple. Human psychology was too complex for simple parallels like that. He knew enough to know that. He was nothing like his mother. She was a noble person and he was a slob—difference number one. He wasn't really. Talking like that was defeatist. He wasn't what one might call a *striking* man but his diet was taking inches off his waist and he was playing squash regularly. Or fairly regularly. He was well read. He needed new clothes: admitted.

Still in many ways he was tempting bait. He did accept that he had to be more . . . aggressive. Had he been so with Donna he might have gained the day. There was, too, his awkwardness. Awkwardness about simple things. Things you can't talk about with people. Like holding a girl's hand. He never felt as though he was holding a girl's hand correctly. These were the bloody things no one ever taught you! Or at least no one had ever taught *him*. He was always conscious of the hands, his palm always sweated, his arm felt too long, and he worried about whether he was holding it too lightly or too tightly. He always sweated. The girl inevitably took her hand away, from discomfort, he supposed. He was relieved when this happened and he could wipe his hand secretly on the inside of his pocket. Again, putting his arm around a girl in a movie never seemed right or comfortable. As the years had passed and he had become older, more conservative perhaps, and especially now that he was a lecturer and no longer a tutor or undergraduate, he felt that it was somehow undignified for him to have his arm around a girl in a movie. It was somehow adolescent, as well as being uncomfortable. Kissing was an ordeal. He didn't know whether other men found it so, but he certainly did. He never knew whether the girl wanted to be kissed. How the devil did one *know*? Sometimes he looked closely at their eyes and sometimes closely at their mouths. Sometimes he thought he could tell but they were rare. He had asked the worldly Bernard about it once after spending a night with him—one of those "male encounters" which he had stopped a year and a half ago. Bernard had laughed. Bernard was sophisticatedly bi-sexual and could afford to laugh. He had said "play it by ear"—typically inexplicit. All very well, but most women were so uncommunicative. They didn't give you a clue about what they wanted. Usually he finished up saying goodnight and inventing some excuse for dashing off. Usually he went to his club to drink frustrated beers. He had on occasions persevered and invited girls to his flat and made conversation and coffee.

Sitting on the sofa trying to put one's arm around a girl is damned ungraceful. When one has a cup and saucer in one's hand it is downright dangerous. There was the light too. It was embarrassing to have a full light blazing when you were trying to . . . pet. He had thought about having a more subdued light but then it would be so obvious what it was all about. He would be self-conscious because the girl would know and he would know she knew. Then there was the filling-in of the time at which he had become, in his own opinion, highly proficient. He was pretty good at conversation and could talk for hours. He supposed it was his academic experience. His intelligence had served him well on occasions but not so well on others. Once he got going he was safe. Stopping was a more difficult matter. Usually the girl said she must be going or that it was time for bed. When they said that it was time for bed he often wondered if it wasn't a veiled invitation to him to make love. He often wondered there and then, and later, about it. He tried to weigh the nuance of meaning in it. But he never arrived at a sure enough assessment at the time to act upon it. There had been a nurse he had taken out whom he'd been sure had wanted him to make love to her. She had been quite aggressive. *She* had kissed *him*. And she had put her hand on his knee, almost above the knee. He had looked down to see— he realised now that this was the wrong thing to have done. He shouldn't have looked down like that. She had been verbally very forward and unsubtle and this had been off-putting. She was just too coarse by his standards. He had the right to discriminate! Well, he drew the line at her type. Not that he would have physically minded going to bed with her but he couldn't bring himself to it because of her manner. It was, frankly, a little frightening. He had dreamed about going to bed with her and even had day dreams too. But that was what he meant—this was not good for him. She, in her own way, was *diverting* him by leading to masturbation. This was the crux of the matter. Girls like that were bad for him. Prostitutes were the same. He'd given them up three years ago. But still they lounged around his mind. Not that he was blaming the sexy nurse or the prostitutes—it was essentially *his* problem and *his* lack of will-power which was diverting him. Yet it was nothing he couldn't overcome if he applied his mind to it. He had always been able to overcome personal defects. His overweight problem for instance. He was capable of completing huge stints of work. He could mark a huge pile of papers or finish a dull book once he had set his mind to it. He even enjoyed setting himself a colossal stint and doing it. He often rewarded himself on these occasions, quite unforgivably, by masturbating. But he could stop that and substitute something more healthy. He had used will-power to stop going to prostitutes and to avoid the occasional "male encounter." He would use it to stop his masturbation. He had to expose himself to female company. That was not as easy as it sounded. Undergraduates were out on ethical grounds—unlike some of his colleagues, he had ethics. Female academic staff were either married or physically unacceptable. The administrative staff in the department were uninteresting. The Historical Society offered nothing. He could theoretically join a mixed social club. But he was not, thank God, a joiner. He had always depended on chance meetings like the nurse who had sat next to him at the theatre. But there was the hotel in town where he had gone with Peterson on a couple of Fridays. He had noticed women there. Probably intellectuals. Of course, money was one of his problems too. It was all very well for people to say, when he complained about money, that he was in a high income bracket. He had the car to pay off and he was helping Mother finance her home unit. He wanted to buy a home unit himself. He was determined not to live with Mother, come what may. He knew enough about psychology to know that was unhealthy. Then he had to keep his number three account going—this was for a definite and personal purpose—never to be financially dependent on anyone. Of course, it would be cheaper to live with Mother and take her unit when she passed on. But she had quite a few years ahead of her yet. It was selfish of him to let her live alone but it was his life after all. Anyhow, true, money was not a *pressing* problem. The important thing was his masturbation. He had another good reason for stopping. It was what he felt to be the mentally *debilitating* effect of it. He was becoming demoralised in the real sense of the word. He was becoming prone to all sorts of thoughts and fantasies which he recognised as definitely mentally unhealthy. And they were *immoral.* Although he was in no way what one could call an orthodox Christian—like his Mother—he did, however, believe in God and if anything was holy and should be kept pure it was one's sexual life. He had day-dreams about being in women's underwear, of wearing jewellery, gold bands on his arms and legs, of being manhandled and slapped by a strong homosexual. These things could eventually be serious and make him mentally ill. He was sure of this. He sometimes wanted to dress in women's clothing and make love to a woman. It was just this sort of thing which was dangerous—these sort of thoughts. He had to get control of this part of his life. Everything else about his life was under reasonable control. His paper for the annual conference of the Historical Society was well under way. He had finished an article for the Journal and a senior lectureship was offering at Monash although he loathed the idea of leaving. He had only to master his sexual problem. If he stopped masturbating his natural male drive would build up and he could go then to the hotel—without Peterson, preferably, although perhaps he would need introductions. If his male drive was strong enough he wouldn't, and he could walk up to a woman and talk to her. Once he got going he would be right, his natural male drive would carry him along. He had wasted it up to now. It seemed such a simple thing to have neglected for so long. He was trained in hindsight: his weakness. It was a matter of Will Power + Natural Sex-Drive + Intelligence + Personal Organisation (like getting his shoes half-soled and heeled) + a little more . . . Aggression together would = Sexual Success. He would find a new way to polish his glasses. A more . . . aggressive way. He would pay attention also to the way he smoked. And other things like that.

Lou Shouted "Hey!"

I WAS IN THE Fortune of War Hotel wondering how I got to be twenty-three. I could remember being eighteen and nineteen and then it became sort of vague. I couldn't remember being twenty or twenty-two and I didn't feel different now I was twenty-three. It was odd because when you had a birthday people always said: How does it feel to be such-and-such an age. I thought that perhaps after being young all the years felt the same. Beside me, Lou and Paul made part of the noise which filled the pub. They were saying something about how it was smart to spring the truth on someone in a difficult conversation. They were saying it was smart to admit you were wrong now and then because people trusted you. I had fallen out of the conversation, or they had pushed me out, about a middy ago, but I was still being dragged along by what I heard of what they were saying. People seemed to curl in and out the bar, like smoke, bringing in new smells. Hair-oil smells, sweat smells, dry-cleaning smells, tobacco. Then there were the smells of beer, spirits, and the rest. I wasn't feeling sick from beer but I wasn't feeling very well either. I remembered that Marj never admitted she was wrong in a conversation. I supposed that came from being an infants' teacher. You think of funny things when you're drinking and I thought about whether Marj would wash my underpants when we were married. I couldn't imagine it. We'd been going together for nearly two years and I bet she'd never thought of my underpants once. I laughed aloud. I often thought of hers. Lou and Paul looked around at me and then went on with their conversation.

Then I watched the man in the blue suit with an RSL badge on his lapel. He was weaving through the smoke and people towards us. Towards me. I said to myself that I must be the type that bar flies always picked to bite. It must be that some faces are sucker faces and the bar flies can pick them.

He reached us soon after his words.

"Got enough for a brandy, mate?" He said, and then he reached us. The others didn't hear him and I looked blankly at him sideways from my beer.

"Got enough for a brandy—for an old Digger and a good trade union man?" he said. He looked nearly drunk and had a beggar-smile. His suit was a Salvation Army handout, for sure.

"Christ!" Lou said as he heard the bar fly. He didn't say it at the man but he said it because he was irritated by the man.

The old man continued his spiel and Lou and Paul turned around.

"I served in the war in New Guinea, mate. They were bloody hard times and I thank the Christ that you won't have to go through it."

I reached into my pocket for money but Lou stopped me by putting his hand on my arm.

He said: "What's this crap about trade unions? You're on the bludge."

I could tell that Lou was going to put the knife into the man.

"Look, mate," the old man said, screwing his eyes narrow and steadying himself with one hand on the bar. "Look mate, you want to know why I'm a trade union man do you? Well, here's why." He cleared the phlegm from his throat.

"I was the best hatter around the place. I made hats with the best of them. I've made top hats for Members of bloody Parliament. Then the Depression came. You're too young to remember that—but I remember. Too-bloody-right I do. We went on strike, see—the hatters' union—thought we'd get things our way a little. See, we didn't know how big this Depression was going to be. Everyone said it'd be over next week. I was a union rep, see. A good tradesman but a good union man. I could ask my own money in the trade but I was for the union. We was out for fourteen weeks. Lived five of them on bread and dripping. You've never tasted that, I'll bet. But things got worse and when the strike was finished there was no jobs for them who helped organise the strike—or for a lot of others too. A lot of us were out of the industry on our backsides. I worked as a labourer when I could, digging ditches on relief and filling them in again. Built a swimming pool at Parkes too. Always thinking that things would pick up. I still put meself down as hatter on all the bloody forms I had to fill in. I was a tradesman. A man with a craft. Here I was digging filthy drains and carrying boxes. You can grin—smirk away—you're only young. I see you don't give a damn. Well, when things picked up general the hat trade never did. In the Thirties everyone wore hats. Now? No one wears hats. The nearest thing I ever got to the bloody trade again was in army stores during the war. I never got back to my trade and labouring ruined my health. You can't learn a new trade after twenty bloody years. You try taking up a pick and shovel after working in felt for twenty years." He looked down at his hands.

I looked at Lou who was grinning and I couldn't stop myself grinning. I felt bad about it and tried to hide it from the old man. But he saw us.

"Christ," he said at us with disgust. He shook his head and said quietly to himself. "Jesus Christ."

I dug twenty cents from my pocket. The man looked at it and then looked at me.

"Stick it up your fat North Shore arse."

He pushed himself off from the bar and weaved away.

Lou turned to me and said: "You didn't fall for that yarn, did you?" He laughed again. Paul laughed with him.

"It sounded true," I said. I leaned back on the bar.

"It was all bull," Lou said "Ten-to-one there wasn't any such bloody union. Anyway, a man can always earn a living in this country if he wants to." He took a drink of beer. "The whole bloody army from the last war seems to be on the bludge." Lou was a salesman. He ordered another round of beers although I didn't want one. I didn't see what Lou would know about unions, or hats, or the last war. I still felt sorry for the man.

Three days later I was sitting at work feeling what my father would call "disorientated." I had begun to feel this way when composing a sales letter which told people of a great new deal our company was offering on trade-ins. It didn't seem that good to me. And I couldn't keep my desk orderly. Our "good deals" made me think about Lou and Paul and their conversation about winning arguments by admitting you were wrong now and then. I thought about doing this in the sales letter: "Dear Customer, This is a lousy deal we are offering you in appreciation of your past patronage." I grinned and thought of giving it to the sales manager. I thought about the Digger in the pub and the hatters' union. I wondered if the story were true and how I could find out. I would like to prove Lou wrong just once. Just once. I knew a man who lived across the street from us who was a history teacher at the university. I'd talked to him about lawn mowers while we both mowed lawns on Sunday. He seemed the sort of person who might know. I decided to ring him. I was uneasy because the sales manager could hear through the glass partition and he didn't like personal calls.

The university put me through.

"I'm the son of Mr and Mrs Wake across the street. You know, we were talking about mowers last Sunday."

I told him I wanted to know about the hatters' union and the Depression.

"I'm surprised to hear you're interested. Is it for some sort of assignment—technical college or some course?"

I told him it was for a bet.

He said the story sounded plausible but he didn't know details. He gave me the name and telephone number of a man at the Trades Hall who would know. We finished and he said in a friendly way, "Till Sunday".

The union man was fairly cold when I told him what I wanted. I said that it was a university assignment.

"As far as I remember about half the hatters lost their jobs over a period of years up to and after the war," he said. It sounded like a speech. "I was not actively associated with the hatters' union but we of the Federated Textile Workers' Union had connections with them and I was a personal friend of the late state secretary. It was always a tight industry but it's a good deal tighter today. A little like the blacksmiths."

He pretty much backed up the old man's story and that made my day.

I met Lou in the bar next day and told him. He laughed louder and longer than I felt was necessary. I thought he must be laughing while he thought up what to say.

"Jesus," he said. "You're not still worrying about that drunk."

I asked him if he had been bulling about the man.

"Of course I bloody was. What would I know about hats? Can't you tell bullshit when you hear it?" He laughed again.

Maybe it was my mood from the office which was still with me. "Disorientation." It was at first. Then it was the way Lou laughed and what he laughed about. It was because what he laughed about was so like everything we had laughed about for so long.

Then it occurred to me as I stood there in the bar that I was feeling very tired. Tired in a way I'd never felt before. I didn't feel like talking. What Lou said was true. I couldn't tell bullshit when I heard it. And then, I hadn't really thought about bullshit until Lou put it to me that way. How do you tell bullshit? The old man hadn't been talking bullshit. Lou had. How do you tell bullshit?

There was a lot of bullshit around. At work for instance. That bullshit letter.

I put my glass down and puffed out my cheeks. I tried to get an idea of what to say or what to do but the only word which came in my mind was "bullshit." I was feeling very odd, to say the least. Sick in the head as though my brain wanted to vomit. I picked up my glass again and then I realised that Lou and I were both in the bullshit game and making a living at it. The old man was fair dinkum and had to bludge a living. I thought: "That's bloody funny, that is." Then the glass started to slide down my fingers on its moisture. I just let it slide. It dropped out of my hand. Down to the floor and the beer splashed like an explosion on our shoes and trousers. I looked down. The glass wasn't broken. That seemed bloody funny too, for some reason.

I still wanted to cry but not only from the eyes.

"What's the bloody matter with you?" Lou said, angrily brushing the beer from his trousers.

And then I gave the glass a tremendous kick and it shot across the bar floor and smashed against the wall between a man's legs.

Lou shouted "Hey!"

I pushed past a few people and ran. I ran out of the bar and along the street for a block or so.

Since I ran that day two months ago I haven't been back to the pub, to work, to Marj, to Lou, or to anything.

BRAVERY

Walking Out

HOW, IN BED EARLY Thursday morning, do you explain to your father and your mother who you have lived with for twenty-three years, that you do not want to go to work and that you do not want to see your friends? How do you explain that you'd rather not see them, too? How do you explain that the idea of working and the idea of seeing your friends makes you feel sick in the head? How do you explain that you want to lie down somewhere on your own?

So I lay on my back in bed early Thursday morning knowing that the clock was ticking towards seven o'clock and that at that time my mother would call me, saying "Thomas, Thomas," as if she worked by the cogs and springs of the clock. Some mornings I thought that if I stopped the clock Mother would stop.

I didn't know why I wanted to lie somewhere by myself, like a sick cat. It didn't sound reasonable to say to anyone. Having something strange to do or say always bothered me and I would rather shrug out of it if I could. But this time I wasn't going to do that. I told myself that when I stopped work I could loaf about. And this was just what I wanted to do because I'm a lazy bastard at heart. Reading was one thing I hadn't done much of since school. Always other things on. I liked a good story — something like "Peyton Place" and I wouldn't mind reading "Lady Chatterley's

Lover" if I could get hold of a copy. There were a lot of movies I wanted to see.

"Thomas, Thomas," cried my mother. I looked at the clock: seven o'clock — bang on. This morning I was fresh when I heard her call instead of dull.

I propped up on my elbow and looked around the room. Pennants of school football.

A pile of magazines — *Playboy* hidden at the bottom. In the cupboard I knew that there was a box of broken toys. The wardrobe was full of clothes. On the door hung a camera bag and camera worth $250 — it used to be my hobby. A speargun leaned in a far corner partly behind the wardrobe. I knew my mother had pushed it behind the wardrobe because it frightened her. It was worth a few bucks too. A window overlooked our lawn where I had spent the last ten years of Sundays mowing. There was a picture on the wall of two nude boys warming their arses in front of a coal fire. On the dresser was a big flagon nearly full of cents and two cents which was once a saving for a car and then for going overseas. When Lou had decided not to go I had pulled out. Now it was for the marriage. Marj always put money in it when she came over.

Marj. I wormed back in the bed away from thinking of her. I guessed she was part of it all. Part of my mother and father and work and Lou and the whole lot. We'd had beaut times, Marj and me, but Christ she drove me up the wall at other times. Then I realised that I had not let the thought about her driving me up the wall come into my head before, or if I had, I more or less pretended that I hadn't seen it. I'd hidden away from the idea. The more I thought about Marj the more I realised that she was a silly bitch. She knew every-bloody-thing. I loved her though, I guess. I told her I loved her every time we went out. It seemed that it always came out when we were kissing and loving up. That's when it always happened. Perhaps I didn't really love her. I nodded to myself in bed and felt relieved that the idea of not loving her had come into my head and stayed. My brain had never really let in ideas against Marj before. My brain keeps telling lies. No, it wasn't always like that — I hadn't been game enough to ask my brain direct questions. Of course, I'd known my brain was lying but I'd been too weak to stop it. It was easier to let it use me and my mouth. Easier to stay in the rut of a lie, like driving. I'm two people, I thought, one of me is a liar and the other is a coward. What a splendid combination. I lay face down in the bed and enjoyed condemning myself.

When Marj and I would be talking or sitting about at home she would often start saying how it would be nice to live in this suburb or that suburb and she would cut plans of houses out of the Sunday papers. Now I knew that I'd never really believed that I'd live in one of those houses with her.

We usually had a fight if we were sitting around with nowhere to go. I used to listen to the way she talked with Mother too. Some of the things didn't mean anything. I think they only talked to let each other know they were still in the room.

We'd never had any real sex either. Just playing around. When I did get her to use her hand she would always say after that she had been carried away. She'd lie there looking depressed and sinful as if something putrid had happened. And she wanted to wipe her hand as quickly as possible. Other fellows' girls would be in it. And then there was her makeup. I couldn't understand why she wore makeup so thick. I thought she looked all right without it. She would only laugh when I mentioned it. She'd say: "Oh, you're a boy and you wouldn't understand." I thought it was supposed to be worn because it pleased boys.

I heard Mother coming along the hall. She looked her gray head in.

"Time to get up, Thomas. Father's up."

Father was always up. How could I tell her? She would be puzzled and scared. Father would come. He would ask what all the nonsense was about me not going to work. He'd be quivering around the lips.

"Are you all right?" my mother asked, puzzled by the way I was looking. She came into the room and peered down at me, putting her hand on my brow.

"You have a temperature," she said.

"I'm feeling sick," I said. "I don't think I'll go to work today." And then I felt wild for having said that instead of saying what I really wanted to say.

"It could be the flu—it's going around."

"Yes, I think it's the flu," I said, and rolled over away from her—tired from knowing how easily I bullshitted.

"I'll bring you your breakfast in bed. I'll get something from the chemist when I go up the street later."

"I'm not hungry."

"You must eat. I'll bring you a poached egg," and she straightened the bed clothes and left.

I had to clamp my mouth to stop from shouting at her that I didn't want a fucking egg. I was racked with the feeling that I wanted to jump up and run out of the house in the same way I'd run out of the hotel and away from Paul and Lou. Again I had the same feeling throwing up inside me. I had smashed my beer against the wall of the pub and run out. I smiled as I saw it all and Lou and Paul standing with amazement on their faces.

Now that the feeling was coming again. I wanted to get away from the endless bloody conversations which tried to make me do what I didn't want to do. They just beat me down until I said yes for peace and quiet. Plans for me to settle down when I didn't want to settle down. Get up in the morning when I didn't want to get up. Writing letters at work that said things I didn't want to say to people I didn't want to say them to. Bullshit letters. Poached eggs I had to eat when I didn't want to eat them. I felt they were dragging me by the legs over a gravel road. But I was going to kick my way free. I wasn't going any further with them.

Father was at the door.

"What's the matter with the young lord?" he boomed. He was dressed for work. Blue suit. Shoes spit polished, army style. He was doing his tie as he stood there. Chin pointed up.

"Feeling a bit of Thursday sickness?" he said.

Mother was behind him. "He's got the flu, I think." My Father laughed. "That's what I call the typists' sickness. They have flu a day or two every month." He laughed. "Never seen a man with it yet." He laughed some more.

"Father, you're naughty," my mother said, leaving the room to cook my unwanted poached egg which I would stuff down my unwilling neck.

"When you take sickies they find out that you're not wanted," my father said, walking down the hall to the bathroom. "You'd better watch out," he shouted. Chuckling, chuckling, chuckling.

Oh Christ, not one more day of this. I was twenty-three. Not one more day of this.

Then, depressingly, I knew that I was weak. Weak as shit. I wouldn't do it. Before going to sleep I had the idea of getting a flat. I had my pay for the week and $800 in the bank. I could live for a fair while without working. Bugger it, I thought, I will do it. I got up and went to the kitchen and picked up the *Herald*.

"You get back to bed," my mother said. "You can't be very sick if you want to read the paper."

I stuck my thumb at her in the hall where she couldn't see.

As I was about to get into bed my father appeared at the door of the bedroom again.

"Come on son, you're not sick."

I turned to him. I felt weak standing in my pyjamas in my bedroom filled with things which made me feel as young as a boy. My heart beat fast. Answering Father back had always been difficult.

"I'm not going to work today," I said, quiet and strong.

"What?" he said, although he heard me.

"I'm not going to work today."

"But you're not sick," he said.

"I know," I said, almost firmly, "but I'm not going to

work today." Shaking a little I lay down on the bed and spread the paper out and pretended to read it.

"You're a damn fool," he said angrily. "You'll find out that playing around doesn't pay off." He walked off. I felt as though I had won something. But I wished I'd told him what I really felt.

I heard him say to Mother: "He's no sicker than my big toe."

My mother said something about me not having had a day off sick for years. No, I thought, not even when I was as sick as a dog. My Father had always talked me into not letting the firm down. Shit.

I saw that there were plenty of flats advertised in the paper. I ate the poached egg almost gagging on each spoonful. I heard my father taking his careful steps along the path to work. I heard my mother washing up and singing. Heard her ring the office and tell them I was sick. Heard her carpet sweep the lounge room.

At about eleven my mother went out to shop. I showered and dressed. As I was doing my hair I started to whistle and I felt strong in my clothes. I felt free because everyone else was at work and that I had my own plans for once and my day was my own for once.

I put on my transistor and the blare of the music scared away a spider of uneasiness on my stomach. I looked at my face in the mirror and picked a pimple. Noticed dandruff in my hair. Still from about three feet away I looked almost boyish. I noticed the skin under my jaw was starting to droop. Jesus, a fellow would be old before he knew what happened to him.

I took my bank book and looked at the figures $800. I kissed it. I packed an airline bag with a few casual clothes and things I would need. I found my sheath knife at the bottom of the drawer. I put it in because it was somehow good to have. I decided not to take any aftershave lotion. It smelt of going to work.

I looked around the room to see if there was anything else I wanted to take and as I did I felt weakened and pushed down by the memories in the room. I turned up the transistor and the music scared away the memory spiders too. My eyes read a framed saying on my dressing table:

"This above all: to thine ownself be true, And it must follow, as the night the day, Thou canst not then be false to any man."

As I read it I thought it was a beaut saying. It was bloody true. I thought that I would take it with me. It was a twenty-first birthday present from my uncle, who was a Rotarian. I read it again and a bloody strange thing happened. I read half way through it and as though someone had scrambled the words it didn't make sense. I tried to read it again. I knew what it meant one minute and the next I didn't. Or had I known what it meant at anytime? I tried to work it out. I supposed it meant that you had to tell yourself when you were bullshitting. If you did this then you wouldn't bullshit to others. But this wasn't right. Sometimes a thing was bullshit at one time and not another. I told Marj I loved her when we were loving up and I meant it. But this morning for instance, it had been bullshit. It was hard to catch yourself being honest. Sometimes I'd be talking and something true would sneak into my head and I would see it but not take any notice. Then it would be gone. Even when I knew I was bullshitting it didn't stop me being false. I was a bullshit artist and I wrote bullshit letters. I was false to every bloody man. I laughed. So I left the saying where it was on the dressing table.

In the dining room I felt weak and knew I could never face my father or mother. So I told myself I was coward and wrote:

"Dear Mum and Dad, I've decided to do a thing which is pretty strange. I'm leaving home for a while. I'm going because I want to be alone. I want to work things out. I'll ring you. If Marj calls will you tell her I'll be seeing her soon. Love, Thomas."

I propped the note on the fruit bowl on the mantlepiece of the dining room. I had to go over the reasons why I was leaving again to get my legs to move. I remembered my dry cleaning and wondered if I should pick it up. I remembered that Lou would call for squash on Monday night. I thought about the housekeeping money and pulled out four dollars. I wrote on the note: "P.S. Here is the housekeeping money. I'll pick up my dry cleaning."

I took an apple from the fruit bowl, picked up my bag, walked through the kitchen and outside down the path. The front gate had an enamel plate on it saying "Beware of the dog" but we hadn't a dog for ten years. My mother said dogs caused too much grief. They were either hit by cars or they ran away. Ran away, I thought, and grinned. Not only dogs.

Chewing apple, I walked along the streets of hedges, trees and lawns. I looked at the lawns and gardens and thought about the work involved in them. If there were 365 lawns and gardens in the street it would mean that about a hundred years of work would be sweated away every four years. A hundred years of life. But no more of my sweat would go to fertilise the lawns.

I was feeling free but nervous. It was no use lying to myself. Unto thine ownself etc. I was nervous because I didn't know what I'd be doing tomorrow or the day after or the day after. Perhaps I was feeling lonely already. I thought about Marj. What would I say to her? Then I laughed because at that moment I realised that I had no intention of seeing her again. I was walking out on my job, my parents, my girlfriend and every bloody thing. I was cold inside my stomach as though it was raining there. But I wasn't going back. Of that I was sure. I'd left all right. I laughed aloud and then the bus came along loaded with silent, hunched people.

But in the bus I knew that I had been laughing to hear myself. Like Marj and Mother. Making noises to show myself I was still there.

I Saw a Child for the Three of Us

I HEARD BERNARD talking but I did not listen to all his words, only to the flow of his talk. To the pace and tone of the sounds, which said that he was at ease. He was at ease because of our natures and what they had created between us. I realise it now. Between us there were no laid-down expectations and nothing necessarily to be done or said from being together. We were not old lovers living on those habits which occasionally delight but which leave nothing to remember. And nor were we new lovers with those anxious gropings and that clumsy hurry. But nor did we have one of those almost-intimate friendships made up of words but with each person trapped behind a sort of high fence of asexuality. We were in some ways brother and sister but with the deeper touchings of sexuality. Like brother and sister because what brought and held us together for the brief times, out of the turmoil, was as inescapable as blood. It was, I realised, Bernard's sexual nature and my crippled feelings and what they had done to us. It was because somehow, perhaps accidently, we had seen each other's wounds and embraced each other from pity and identification and for comfort in our sexual darkness.

There was a knowing that we were almost true with each other, as true as minds can dare, and unashamed of what we knew about each other. Whatever we concealed from each other, and the small distortions, came because we couldn't bear the way it would hurt for some of the things to pass out and also from wanting to make things better, for wanting to make things better for each other—better than true.

I knew that desire, if stirred, would be quiet and not ravenous, not like a tumult, but a subdued, consciously done thing. Ravenous and tumultuous sex we had both had, not together, but with others, and it was splendid too, but it did not belong with us. Our sex was a caress, not a physical dazzle.

Then I was aware of the objects around us in the room—the heavy, burnt coarse clay of the ashtrays, the squat glasses, and the pottery flagon. They were beautiful to us and significantly present, contributing, but not intruding. The wine we were drinking was tempered and was kissing our nerves, sinews, and muscles to a hush.

And Bernard was saying: "And it's nothing bad about Mervyn and me that makes me want to be with you. But I suppose it must be in a way. If things were perfect with Mervyn and me I suppose I wouldn't want anyone else, would I?"

And I replied: "Perhaps not. But perhaps the idea of one person being enough is wrong for some people. Perhaps some people should look for three-person affairs. Or perhaps it just happens to some people."

"But Mervyn and I are happy. We have our fights—but what people who live together don't? The neighbours keep to themselves but they say hullo. I don't think they know we are camp. Except the girl in flat four—the dancer I was telling you about—I think she knows we are camp. She's always very 'girlie' with us, you know? She's not a square. But it's been good. Did you realise that we'd been living together for over a year now? Yes, it's that long. Remember how I was? Sometimes I'd be taking a girl out and then the next week I'd be at the Rex looking for a boy. Oh, those dreadful one night stands. God, I was miserable. You remember how I'd come knocking at your flat in the middle of the night and cry on your shoulder?"

"It made me feel as if I could mother you. Remember that sometimes your body forgot you were camp and I used to tease you about it."

And Bernard wondering about me.

"I have men. But living with John ruined me. It's a tremendous effort to take an interest in another person. And it's more than two years since we split up. Perhaps I've used up my passion, perhaps you only have so much. Every new affair reminds me of John. It's cruel because so many things repeat themselves in an affair—expressions and situations. We aren't very original about love. We all say and do just about the same things. I don't think I can really try anymore. Or care."

. . . me . . . gay Terri . . . bubbling my life away for what and for whom . . . like a boiling pot on a stove with nothing to cook . . . evaporating my life . . . carefully making up my face, carefully dressing, every day, for whom and for what? . . . choosing beautiful clothes for whom? . . . cleaning the flat and re-decorating it . . . the new meetings with new men and the expectations and the slow fading of the affair . . . the tiresome efforts to be thoughtful and to feign pleasure . . . for how long and why?

Bernard saying that everyone wants love and we look too furiously and we scramble over each other and instead of love we make sexual scratches and we don't mean to hurt. But we do.

. . . darkness. Quietness. John. Tearfulness. Tomorrow. Alone in a double bed with someone. Showering. Sad drinking. Mad laughing . . .

I reach out and hold Bernard's hand. We kiss lightly. We move to the bed and lie down together.

"To your boyish part I'm a mother and to your male part I'm a lover and to your feminine part I'm a girl friend."

Sometimes people take off their clothes but even then aren't naked. Bernard and I are always naked.

In the warmth that had stayed after the day's hot sun, next to the slim, longhaired girlish boy cradled childlike in my arms I thought of a child. I felt with my mind that feeling of explosion which I imagined was the way conception happened. I felt it in me by thinking it. Then I wanted it. I wanted to be feeling it with my body. But more than the having of the child I wanted to feel the movement of life in me. To know the workings of my unwake body. How would it be once it was lit? To not waste the coming of lovemaking but to allow it to work into me. To have it work its way into me and combine with me and fire me with a child. I'm sure the smell from me would be richer and heavier if my body was let free. To be stoked hot. Sometimes in the rush of loving I'd wish that the boy, whoever he was, would not fumble for safety but would allow himself to come free and pulsating into me and to allow us to mingle freely so that I would then have in me a baby.

Now as the male in Bernie stirred and I felt it pressing against my thigh, I saw a child for the three of us. For Mervyn, Bernie and me. And we would raise the child and love it. And I would need no more lovers because it would love me as its mother. I would live my life for my baby.

With my fingers and breasts I coaxed Bernie into leaving his man-woman world for a shortwhile.

"Don't worry about that, Bernie. Just love me. Don't worry about that . . . just love me . . . just let yourself be free and forget . . . just love me."

And he said: Yes, Terri. Yes, Terri. All right.

"Give me a child, Bernie, give me. Give me. Be free, so free with me . . . be free . . ."

. . . and he came to me as a male for the brief flickering maleness that was in him. I roused it and I took it. And I knew that he would subside again into a land I could only go to as a visitor. But I didn't mind. And now if nature agreed there would be a new person made for us to love. And he would be a child for the three of us.

Ten Years

AS ALWAYS, after an invitation, the two boys inside him wrestled: the boy who said go for the kicks and the chance of a screamingly exciting night; the other boy who said that it would be dreary and embarrassing and that the habit should be kicked. As almost always, the first boy won, and he had accepted the invitation.

The difference this time was that the invitation came from Terry who went back ten years. Terry had been the sophisticated young doctor. Commanding in social situations, sure in social practice, witty, a theoretical nineteenth century conservative with a passion for T. S. Eliot. A person who was a victim of his own assurance—inflexible and reluctant to venture far from the standard situations he knew.

What had *he* been ten years ago? A golden young boy. Well tanned, wild blonde hair, gay blue eyes. Full lips with a tendency to pout. Some natural grace. All physical—socially trading on his body. Instead of a personality he had a perverted sensitivity which allowed him to adapt quickly and falsely to any company—to merge with the company. He fancied he did this less now. He had been a golden boy who had just passed his teachers' college exams and knew nothing. He had read one poem by T. S. Eliot and didn't remember it and knew no politics and did not care for it—until he had to please others who did. His social training had been the minimum given by the home of a country shopkeeper. He had behaved in a way which, had he been two years older, Terry would have described as gauche, but which he had accepted then, graciously, as youthful awkwardness. After a faux pas, then, Terry simply ruffled his hair and corrected him. Two years later he would have shown wordless, cold irritation in company and slapped him later in private. For a while he had resisted Terry sexually, preferring to enjoy his food and talk—learning about wines, cheeses and manners, but refusing his bed.

"I don't want to, that's all. No reason. I don't have to give a reason."

Terry avoided the absolutely direct proposition and so avoided loss of face. He was sure that Terry had often been at the point of pleading or breaking into anger. But always he was able to say in his quiet careful way: "Never mind. It is not important (a lie). But it puzzles me, why not? You say you have no moral objections and that you have been to bed with other men. And you know my feelings for you. And you trust me. Why not?" Terry would draw lightly on his thin cigar, his voice carrying only the slightest suggestion of impatience.

From him—an uncomfortable flush. Struggling to say no in some convincing way. But without a rational no. Becoming petulant. Escaping from reason to the demonstrative. The flouncing, the nasty, the abusive. Girlish—the stylised, unconscious camp imitation. He was always surprised how natural and easy his girlishness was. It was truly a part of him even if it did appear affected to some. Bugger them. It was with Terry that he had first realised that he could use his lips and eyes expressively. Terry had brought it out in him.

Now it was ten years past. No longer the golden boy. In the mirror he had noticed wrinkles. He had told himself they were becoming, marks of world-weariness. Although perhaps he was that to a degree. It was one of his poses. Also on his face was a certain . . . dishonesty?—for those who suspected it. Also some signs of *calculation* hiding behind lines of posed ingenuousness. He could be open but he did have a mind which calculated the percentages and his spontaneity was so often phoney. Perhaps his inner conflict about his way of life showed too. The conflict was no longer fierce and he was resigned to his sexually mixed—confused?—existence. He really didn't care anymore. He thought at times he was less camp now but on the other hand he was more fluent and easy when camp. He got-off less now. Or did he? Perhaps it just seemed that way. Perhaps he should keep a list.

Soon after he had begun to sleep with Terry he had been shifted to the staff of a country school. They lost contact after a couple of letters and he had learned, for the first time, the shallowness of affairs, something he had since come to accept. But perhaps all affairs fade quickly when the sex is gone—despite everything everyone says at the time.

Now the chance meeting and the dinner invitation. They were in each other's physical reach again.

He wanted to go to bed with Terry this time without a doubt. Time had given Terry elegance. He was supple and well kept. ("You've looked after your figure, darling.") Now so much more commanding. One could be so much more passive with him because he was so much stronger.

DURING THE DINNER they talked of before.

"I had not realised," Terry was saying, "although it had crossed my mind on occasions, that Peter was camp. Now after ten years I find out. One doesn't ever know."

"I now assume everyone is camp until proved otherwise." That amused Terry.

Terry talked of having loved an Italian boy named Felix and how the boy had trampled him (or "tramped" him, as Terry joked). The usual story of theft, cruel bitter argument, fights and breaking things—in this case the dinner set they had bought for their flat. Times of utter devotion. It was all over now.

He watched Terry's eyes and saw the strength—boasted by his eyebrows. The hands with nails so carefully kept. Virile hands with virile white hairs bushed on the backs of his fingers. He sat there feeling that Terry could not have failed to receive the signals of his eyes: Let's stop talking and go home. Ask me home. Take me home. Take my arm and propel me—to your bed. Undress me. I'm not the golden young man but I'm attractive—I've been told enough times to believe it. I still feel the same. My voice in bed is soft and husky like a boy. I've strong, smooth legs . . .

But Terry talked of art. Terry talked of having settled. Bought a home unit—"In which I shall probably live until I die." He had investments. He talked economics. Terry was in command of his life.

"But what I don't possess—is a good intimate friendship.

I'm not talking of one-night stands. I'm talking about a really serious living together. I want something that grows and lasts and can be worked at. It's three years since Felix and he didn't understand. I'm sick to death now of one-night stands. Do you know what I mean?"

"Good God, Terry—you sound as though you're talking of marriage."

"It would be like that—sharing things, growing together. I'm not going to marry a woman of course, that would be inflicting an injustice—but I think it can be achieved by two people who want the same thing."

"Take me to bed and we'll talk about it," he said—just too flippantly. Recognising it just too late.

Terry showed a tiredness, a disappointment.

"I don't want us to sleep together tonight, Bernard. I have talked openly with you because we were very close before and could be again. I've not enjoyed being with someone as much, for a long time."

This made him feel acutely aware that his behaviour that night had been mostly a pose. He felt a shit.

"I want you to ring me next week if you feel that anything can come of our being together—and I think something can —very much I do. I feel we were always suited to each other. But I want you to know what I want from life and how serious I am about it."

He nearly said: "Yes, something can come of us" so as to get to bed with Terry but he for once shied away from dishonesty, swallowed his frustration and said something else.

Terry drove him home then and they touched as they said goodnight.

He had recognised Terry's talk of a serious affair—the big deal—he'd heard it before from men and women. He knew the theory and wasn't interested. He was saddened by Terry's hopelessly formalised way of going about it. How many other casual men had he invited to share his dream?

By a low light he drank a gin and tonic. He remembered that Terry had introduced him to gin and tonic ten years ago. He realised that he was now the age Terry had been then. He had moved from timid youth to the frantic sexuality of mid-twenties—so often grabbing at one-night stands with both clutching hands. But Terry had moved onto a mellow time. There was no place for him in the mellow time. It was a desperate mellow time. And it was ahead, of course.

The Train Will Shortly Arrive

THE TRAIN WILL be arriving in approximately five minutes. Would passengers wishing to alight from the train at this station please move to car five. The train will stop at the platform for approximately one minute. Thank you.

In the rocking train toilet he tried to do *something* with his hair. He smoothed it down with water. He sighed. They were just going to have to put up with it. It had been trimmed and shaped. It wasn't as though it was *scruffy*. It was just *long*. He pulled a face at himself and began to move unsteadily along the corridor to his seat. No-one would look twice in the city but in the town . . .

"Your stop next," the bore next to him said, in case he'd forgotten.

The trained stopped, and stood making those impatient steaming noises. "All right, I'm getting off, don't rush me," he said. He looked around for his mother or father although his mother had written to say they couldn't meet the train because they had visitors. He went to a cab drowsing at the curb.

He got in. *Rylands Cabs for fast reliable service. Radio controlled. Twenty-four hours a day. Telephone 2343*. He gave the driver the address. The driver knew it.

"You'd be Fred Turner's son—young Bernie—," the driver said, screwing around to look at him.

He nearly denied it for no particular reason.

"Yes. I'm home on a visit."

The cab driver gave him another glance. Glanced at his hair, his sunglasses, his bracelet and then started the cab.

Satisfied?

"You've changed. I remember you as a kid. You wouldn't remember me."

"I do. I remember you but I don't remember your name."

"Jack Ryland. I run a couple of cabs."

Jack Ryland pulled a card from the upholstery trim above the driver's seat and without looking passed it back to him.

"You were a tough little bugger."

What a lie.

"But that'd be going back to when you were about ten. What you be now? Around thirty?"

"That's close enough." How coy.

They drove up the drive of the house. Ryland helped him out with his bag. His parents must have heard the car and they came out to the front porch. His father peering through his reading glasses. Why did he always, but always, wear the wrong pair? His mother was wiping her hands on her apron.

His mother hugged him and they kissed. He shook hands with his father, who said hullo to Ryland.

"Your boy's changed, Fred—I mean he's grown."

Oh, for God's sake get off the *changed* bit. His father looked for bags to carry—anything to distract him.

Inside he was introduced to the visitors who were sitting in the lounge room drinks in hand. They struggled to be interested. He felt the dull private alcoholic humour of a group which had been drinking together for some time. He felt the group stir alcoholically in an effort to fit him in.

"Bernie's been overseas. We haven't had him home for years."

He took off his sunglasses.

"How nice for you," one of the women visitors said, then gave a smothered giggle and said: "I mean that he's home again." The others giggled.

"What'll you have to drink son? We got everything." His father opened the stocked drink cabinet which was lined with mirrors and lit up when the door opened.

"Let Bernie wash his hands dear," his mother said.

"No, have a drink—first things first," his father said, looking to the visitors who laughed accordingly.

The cabinet's range had expanded. Before it had been rum and sherry. The store must be prospering.

"Come on dear," his mother said to him, picking up her sherry. "I've put you in your old room." She guided him out. How much sherry was his mother drinking these days? And how much rum his father? His mother led him off.

"I'll have a gin and dry," he said over his shoulder to his father. He saw his father stare at the cabinet with just the slightest hesitation. "I have some Black and White." For a second he felt like accepting it, to please his father, as a gesture of something, but he didn't. "No, gin and dry would do nicely, thanks Dad."

Out in the hall his self-consciousness slipped away. They were all dull and boozed and he felt clear control. He'd reached a stockade of superiority.

Sherry in hand, his mother led him to his old bedroom.

"You wash and put your things in there while Daddy gets the drinks."

She noticed the bracelet. "What a lovely bracelet, Bernard." He flushed.

"Oh, I bought it . . . for the trip. My blood group's engraved on it," he lied. He twisted it around nervously and moved off to the bathroom.

In the bathroom he was at the mirror again. You vain old thing. He rubbed under his eyes and for a cruel second saw age looking at him.

He came into the lounge room to hear his mother say: "He's been working at one of the private schools in Sydney —Grammar . . . " His mother turned to him as he entered.

"Your drink is on the cabinet," his father said. "Hope you like plenty of ginger ale."

He didn't but there wasn't much he could do about it now.

"No, that's fine."

"I've been telling everyone about your new position," his mother said.

"Not really new—I've been there six months now."

Someone asked him how he liked it. He said that conditions could be better.

"We teachers are becoming worse than farmers with all our complaining and carrying-on," he swizzled his drink.

"You deserve better dear," his mother said, "education is so important." And with that the conversation left him. They talked bowls, business, with the women talking across at each other and the men talking across at each other. Now and then it would all link up coming back together on the same subject. Now and then his mother would make a reference to him or seek his opinion or give him an explanation —lacing him back into the group as best she could.

He went to bed after dinner, bored and slightly tense.

In bed he missed Mervyn. He ran his hands down his body, aware of his masculinity. He took his penis and it grew rigid in his hand. He longed for Mervyn. Mervyn was probably lying in his bed doing the same. In their flat. How long would he and Mervyn last? Another few months? They had both been with girls. Pathetic attempts to make it as a square. They got along. But there were the days when he said: "Go *away,* Mervyn. Fuck off. Leave me *alone.*" Those days of deep angry depression about God knows what. But didn't all people feel that? And there were the days of glorious fun and loving nights. Of waking to feel Mervyn close and hard. Of the delightful relaxation together in front of television after hectic times. The relaxation and pleasure of showering and then going to Mervyn's bed. Of putting his head on Mervyn's chest. The shouting rows were worth that. The flowers they grew together. He remembered Mervyn teaching him how to garden.

He was careful of the sheets. The climax exploded away some of his tension. Immediately after he had a glimpse of his father—distant and puzzled—and of his mother, so unsurely and clumsily devoted and then they passed from his mind with the tension.

Cum was messy after lonely masturbation. With someone there was usually affection and cum was a binding thing and a tangible expression of it. No, that was bullshit. It was sometimes true—but not always true of those drunken promiscuous nights. Sometimes it was then the mess of spent desire. Sometimes it was the mess of guilt. If the guilt anxieties were troublesome then the "tangible affection" baby, became "tangible guilt." Which one wanted to wipe away quickly.

HE AWOKE to the early morning ABC news.

He'd forgotten the early rising Saturday mornings. The big morning at the store.

His father and mother, alcoholically sour, were probably not talking. He knew his mother would bring a cup of tea and shortbread biscuits. He didn't want to get up. All through childhood he had been made to get up, except now and then when his father and mother fought about whether he should be made to work in the store and his mother won. This morning he would not get up.

His mother brought him the tea, and kissed him good morning.

"I'll stay in bed," he said.

"Yes, do that darling. No need for you to get up. Father's in a foul mood."

He drowsed, leaving his tea to grow cold on the bedside table. Later in the morning he arose, ate his breakfast alone, put on his sunglasses and strolled up town.

Saturday morning in the country town. People stood on the sunlit side of the street at the gutter's edge talking about yesterday. Children ran slow messages. Young people swaggered on their bicycles propped against walls. A few early drinkers stood at hotel doorways with their first-of-the-day beers calming the jumping nerves and taking away the bitter taste of last night's sweetness. The adolescents out of schoolclothes flirted with tough aloofness in laminex milk bars. In the Red Rose, the New York, and the Paragon. He'd taken tense girls there after Saturday night movies at the Kings or the Victory for cold milk shakes and later when older, to the coffee shop for sophisticated black coffee and sophisticated raisin toast. He'd liked double dating with Peter best. Mainly because it was reassuring to have male company when one was so unfamiliar and ignorant about girls. But he had liked, or perhaps loved, Peter. He'd not been fully aware, and could not have admitted it, and it could not have been advanced. Only later when they were about twenty and he was beginning to recognise and admit his sexual nature had he recognised what he felt about Peter and it was then too late. Peter was tough and could never have been approached. But there had been a timid, guilty, mutual masturbation at about sixteen. Amazingly spontaneous at its beginning—a sexual urge forcing itself awkwardly, but strongly, through their conventions and inhibitions. It had been at Peter's home. It was left undiscussed. They both feigned sleep immediately after. He must have been staying with Peter that night. Peter's parents were probably away. It had never been repeated and never mentioned. He had dreamed of Peter and thought of him while masturbating in the years since. Had Peter thought of him? He doubted it. Peter had married a Catholic. Of course, Peter hadn't been the first. There had been a younger sexual thing—unselfconscious and pubescent. Of a different nature. Before girls. Girls had been necessary for Peter and him. Necessary for all of them then, for status at school and for curiosity, and so that they could say "I love you" for the first time and feel the first breast since infancy. But oh the tension of it.

He went into the Red Rose and ordered a banana malted. The taste of it made him shiver with memories.

He sat in a stall and watched people as they went by on Saturday business, some he vaguely knew. Some he'd seen fifteen years ago walking by on Saturday mornings as they did now. God how comfortable. Knowing that you'd be doing that on Saturday morning, every Saturday morning. Knowing that there was nothing hostile, hysterical, or dangerous to face in the journey through Saturday. Or perhaps there were horrors in that Saturday journey for some. As they went down the sunlit street some must have feared creditors, had to face forbidden people they desired, face people who held grudges. But weren't his Friday nights and Saturday mornings also ritualistic? But they were frantic—frantic rising late on Saturday morning, frantic hangovers, and hungover shopping with Mervyn at the supermarket with all the other frantic Jews and camps and bedsitter girls. He smiled and wanted to be back in the frantic ritual. It wasn't all *that* depressing and at least one knew one was *alive*. But it didn't have the . . blandness . . . of the country town Saturday.

A man came into the milk bar. No. A boy came into the milk bar. In his mind the man was a boy. The boy, Harrison Bryant, was about thirty—in his mind he remembered him as a soft boy of eleven. The boy had coarsened into a man. It frightened him a little. He could hardly see a trace of the soft boy. Bryant's hair was cropped up to the crown. He had fattened at the waist. His belt pulled tight was his only attempt at control. His clothes were the characterless light greys and fawns. A singlet filled a vee across the neck of his sports shirt. Harrison Bryant's hands seemed frightfully wrinkled. He looked down at his own in shock. But he could not see them as someone else would see them. They seemed as they had always seemed—young and vivacious—if hands could be vivacious. Vanity.

Harrison Bryant wore rubber thongs. He abhorred rubber thongs—ugly, common, and probably harmful to the feet. The thirty-year-old Harrison Bryant was buying a packet of cigarettes and with cupped hands had lit one, dragged on it and emphatically expelled the smoke in a relieved gust, as a smoker who was overdue for a cigarette. He had a gold metal watch band. Against the sun-bleached white hairs of his arm it was the only feature resembling the male attractiveness of youth.

Should he speak? It would be unbearable. But it was intriguing. And wasn't he there for *that* sort of thing—to see some of it again? He wasn't sure whether he wanted to see it all again. But wot-the-hell, archy.

"Harrison," his voice came out light, almost camp. He roughed it up. "Harrison."

Harrison Bryant turned around and saw him. Quickly taking the cigarette from his mouth, smiling widely, he came over. "Bernie, for Christ's sake, it's been a long time." He came over with his hand out. They shook hands. The last time we touched, he thought, was when we were eleven and your hands were on my penis and my hands were on yours. Remember?

"Well, bugger me," Harrison said. "Where've you been hiding yourself? Christ, you've changed." Harrison's eyes made an appraisal.

"I've been overseas," he said. The appraisal sent a fizz of agitation through him. He wished he hadn't spoken. He pulled out a cigarette.

"Have one of mine," Harrison offered.

Never.

"No thanks, Harrison. I've got to like these."

"Fussy—nothing but the best." Harrison grinned aggressively.

"I don't smoke that much," he said. Calm down. Calm *down.* Harrison moved into the stall opposite him.

"Been overseas?"

"Yes, Europe."

"I was going to work in New Zealand but I don't suppose I'll be going now. Four kids and another on the way—what do you think of that? Married?"

"No," he carefully ashed his cigarette, calmer now, "but it sounds as if you've been hard at it." What a coarse expression.

"All my own work—unless the milkman slipped in," Harrison laughed. He smiled involuntarily at the sheer corniness and pride.

"Where do you work, Harrison?"

"Cut out the 'Harrison' bit—Harry—everyone knows me as Harry. You'd be the only one who'd remember that's my real name."

"I like it," he said. Oh shut up.

Harrison laughed nervously. "I'm at the Golden Fleece service station. A fellow called Simpson runs it—you wouldn't know him, he's from Melbourne. I do a bit of panel beating and work the bowsers—you know."

He nodded.

"It's not the best job in the world. I've got ideas about starting my own panel-beating place or getting a station, but you know." Harrison smiled a lost smile.

He nodded. "Who'd you marry, Harry, anyone I'd know?"

"Betty Harris—don't think you'd know her—she would a been a year behind you at school."

He didn't know her.

"You'll have to come up and see us. We got a Housing Commission place up in the new part."

"I'm only up for a day or two."

"Perhaps next time then."

"Yes."

"Anyhow, what you been up to?"

"I teach. At Grammar."

"Posh school."

"Kids are the same anywhere." Except some have richer parents. Which makes all the difference.

"God you've changed. I mean from what you were at school." Harrison laughed, again nervously, in case he had said something wrong, partially realising what he meant, realising what was different.

"We've all changed," he said, defensively.

There was a silence.

"Ever feel like leaving the old town?"

Harrison tried to consider the question. "I was thinking of moving to Goulburn. Wife's mother lives there. But it's not a bad old town."

Another lapse.

Then Harrison asked again: "What do you do for a crust?"

He tried to answer it as a fresh question, rephrasing his answer to avoid embarrassment.

"Teach school."

"Oh yeah—I asked you that." Harrison stubbed out his cigarette uneasily.

"How's Jimmy Hagan?"

"Don't see much of Jimmy. He's on a farm near Captains Flat. He comes back now and then but I don't see him much. At the football sometimes."

"He always wanted to work a farm."

"He's share farming or something."

Harrison went to take out another cigarette but remembered that he'd just finished one. He played with the packet.

"It's hard to realise that we were in infants school together and grew up together," he said, watching Harrison's face.

Harrison laughed and shook his head as if trying to deny it or shake away the embarrassment of his childhood. It was impossible to know if he remembered the sexual game they had shared. He kept shaking his head and laughing. "It's funny how you grow old."

"We're not *that* old yet." Let's not talk about *age*.

"I see your mum and dad about the place. Your dad drinks in the saloon bar down at Cassidy's. That's where I drink. I see him in the saloon bar after work some days."

"Who do you drink with? Any of the boys I'd know?"

"Sonny Buckley—you'd remember him. Lyle Bates? Used to be real fat?" Harrison warmed to safer talk.

He nodded. He remembered them. He remembered them as kids he'd played football with. Who for years seemed to wear a football jersey or football socks whether they were playing or not.

"Why don't you come down and have a drink with us? They'll be down there about now. We all get down there Saturday mornings."

Curiosity tempted him but his discretion grimaced.

"No thanks, Harrison . . . Harry . . . I have things to do."

Harrison didn't repeat the invitation.

Harrison stood up and said that he had to go and to call in if he was up around the Commission area.

Harrison left the milk bar.

He'd left too. His mind had gone back to among the lantana and grape vines grown wild where he and Harrison had crawled and made a hide-out and where one day, on some forgotten pretext, they had taken off their clothes, lain together and fondled each other's penis to erection. This had occurred—how often? Each time had been initiated by some pretext which even at eleven they had needed to justify the innocent, curious, and affectionate reaching out to each other. Then the first ejaculation—Harrison—and the amazement of it. Harrison had called it "spunk" and seemed to know something about it. But there had been fear and boyish bravado and a need to understand it. They had looked in *Pears Cyclopedia*, Arthur Mees' *Children's Encyclopedia,* and the book *Enquire Within Upon Everything*, and dictionaries. They looked for all the taboo words they'd ever heard—penis, prick, cunt, shit, spunk, and masturbate. The dictionary had told them that spunk meant courage. All the books together left them in a mocking darkness. They didn't touch each other after that —as though the signs of manhood had frightened them away from each other into the "proper" sexual distance for men. He'd been frightened too, of losing his courage.

He remembered their young, hairless, vibrant bodies. His penis stirred even now. Oh god, ageing was miserable. And foolish. An unbelievably foolish process.

Football matches came back to him. Rising on cold, frost and mist mornings to travel by bus to football carnivals. The vigour, and the bodies. The closeness of the team. The beautiful smell of the bodies in the dressing room spiced with the smell of liniment. The male heat of the bodies before and after. The dressing room had been an exciting, male place.

He dug and ground the sugar spoon deep into the plastic

sugar container on the table, angry about ageing. The anger drifted away leaving the grim, impotent acceptance.

He thought again about Harrison's abashed reaction to him. How obviously different from other men he must appear and how he sometimes forgot this. Perhaps he'd never quite accepted that he was. Perhaps he had pretended that if he wanted he could conceal it. That no one need ever know. But it wasn't like that anymore. And it wasn't that he had changed. He hadn't *changed.* He'd simply unwrapped himself. That was that.

Drinking a banana malted in the Red Rose and thinking of the ghosts of childhood princes—princes who had become toads—was a disturbing game. Exciting oneself by remembering pubescent experiences was saddening. Next thing he'd be panting after twelve-year-olds and that would be *the end.* The End. Grammar School scandal.

He dragged himself out of the stall. The milk bar was agitated now by loud adolescents who moved restlessly between the juke box and the street. "Juke": of African origin, he'd told his class. He tried to buy his brand of cigarettes but couldn't and settled for Craven A.

He strolled along the sunny side and around the post office corner. A former primary school teacher came towards him erect with the same ageless authority he had twenty years ago. Was *he* like that to *his* pupils? Existing in the limbo especially allotted to school teachers. He felt like speaking but it would be meaningless for them both. Young people were always so aware of their own identity but for teachers, they were simply part of a straggling procession. The teacher passed with his shopping bag.

There had been a teacher later in high school, and a seduction. He remembered the playground stories about the teacher which had come first, and which had kindled him. The breathless, fearful desire which he had felt when first alone with the man in his office. With the inevitability of mutual desire he had become the teacher's special boy—first for his messages, then for his special conversations and then for his special pleasure. The conversations between them had quickly become personal with the teacher asking about his dreams and about his father and mother. Then the fondling. They had been sitting together at a desk one afternoon when the rest of the school had gone to sport. He remembered being asked to report to the teacher's office instead of going to sport and he felt again the wild excitement which had trembled through him.

They had sat at the desk reading figures from a sheet with the teacher checking them off. He had known it would happen. The teacher's hand came down on to his leg. Firmly then caressingly. His body seemed to silently hum changing then to a silent, low urgent moan but the only sound was the sound of his voice intoning the figures. Trying to control his breathing which wanted to break into grunting or panting. Up and down the columns of figures. The teacher's hand working up slowly and warmly towards the screamingly rigid penis. Up his leg to the fly and then firmly stroking the penis through the trousers. Then in the fly and down in through the underpants. When the hand reached his penis and gripped it he had wanted either to bury his head on the teacher's shoulder in erotic surrender or to run run run away from the embarrassment and guilt which swirled way down under the desire and excitement—an excitement ten thousand times as intense as anything he had ever felt before, with Harrison in the childish bushes or with Peter in the furtive bed. The tickling and caressing brought out the first thrusting of a new feeling—the trembling ecstacy of male touch and sexual submission.

He did nothing for the teacher. He did not look at him. He had stopped reading, suspended in the intensity of the hand on his penis. Then the teacher coughed and the hand withdrew and the fly was zipped. Why did he stop? The unejaculated penis subsided in cold disappointment. Why did he stop? The reading began again. His voice took hold of the figures, up and down the pages. Why did he stop? Then the smile and the gathering of the lists when they finished. The gathering of the pencils and the thank you and the teacher's squeeze of his shoulder. Why had he stopped? His legs were unsteady as they had been on rare occasions since when a certain pitch of sexual intensity was reached with strange boys in strange ways in strange flats. Why had he stopped? The brightness of the playground, empty except for the sound of singsong rote learning somewhere from a defaulters' class. He had gone to the toilet and locked himself in a cubicle to cry against the wall from utter frustration. He had been close to rage and couldn't masturbate. He just cried and beat his hand against the terrazzo wall. Why had he stopped?

God, he'd been so attractive then. So golden, so smooth and so sexually hungry. Soft clean blonde hair and clean finger nails—one of the few boys who had clean nails—and not only because his mother insisted. His fully-grown eyelashes and a physical movement light and without conceit.

There had been three other times with the teacher, again wordless and never as blindingly intense and again never to ejaculation. Why had he always stopped? The sexual occasions with the teacher were flashes from the grinding school year. His place as special boy for the teacher had ended when he left at the end of that year to go to another school. It ended with a dull shaking of hands and pleasantries with him hating the teacher for having always stopped. Their friendship was cracked. He could not straddle the distance between them because of the inadequacy of youth. If only the teacher had not stopped and had spoken to him, tenderly, and coaxingly, he could have had him and gone on totally for years. He would never have opted for another school or gone to teachers' college. He would have stayed at that school to be with the teacher.

He stopped feeding the fantasy. Still alive after all those years. He was now away from the town's shopping centre and moving towards its outskirts where it was circled by bush. The teacher had obviously been blocked and hung up. Probably scared to death. Ejaculating would have demanded something, perhaps would have advanced it all further than the teacher was prepared to go. He wondered about himself. Would he one day begin to fondle favourite boys in his classes? He blanched at the risk and was relieved to see an ethical qualm, large and strong, standing in the way.

He had reached the streets which were half sealed with tracks at the edges for horse traffic. He then came to the end of the sealed streets where only curbing and guttering had reached. The beginning of the bush. Houses had marched along the new streets with plumbing, cement footpaths, and curbing running alongside.

The bush had been a place to go. It was, he remembered, at first a frightening place in which one did not go far. Each foray required a mustering of courage which, because of the gang, had become a forced courage which had taken them further than they wanted into unknown territory. But over the years it was explored and then roved. Familiarity came and the bush offered up its facilities—caves for hideouts, trees for lookouts, creeks to swim in, bamboo for blow pipes, berries to eat, and places to lie quietly concealed. There had been birds to kill although he never had—always firing blind hoping to miss. If the others had known that! But perhaps they all fired to miss.

He crouched on a rock and smoked. He had smoked for the first time in this bush. With Jennifer. What was her other name? Sims? Smoking had given him something like a sexual feeling. It wasn't clear. He remembered the dizziness and the forbidden excitement. She had been the only girl among them. He had kissed Jennifer later, around about puberty. It had been in a dark room and he could not see her. Somehow he had found her hand and then felt her lips against his, moist and moving, like some alive animal. His first kiss. Tinged with nausea.

That had been his childhood—sweet uneasiness. He rocked forward, his legs hunched under his chin.

He became aware of his bracelet which had slid down over the back of his hand. "From Mark." Given before Mark had returned to the States on his wandering from girl to girl and from boy to boy. It was not in memory of Mark that he wore it. Their affair had been brief, passionate, but socially difficult because of possessiveness. The bracelet was a reminder of his sexual identity. His sexual identity bracelet. He put it to his mouth and tasted the cold silver. The cold silver of his youth.

"My youth was nothing but a storm, tenebrous, savage,
Traversed by brilliant suns that our hearts harden,
The thunder and the rain had made such ravage,
That few of the fruits were left in my ruined garden."

He threw up his metaphorical eyebrows. His life didn't warrant poetry.

He glanced back through the thin bush to the Commission houses. He saw a sagging woman in woollen slippers hanging washing on a sagging line. Outside another house a man in overalls lay beneath a car, as though submitting to some sexual machine.

Was that woman Mrs Bryant? She was straightening up, bracing herself against her pregnancy. A child crawled around her feet. He let himself believe it was. Made himself feel a devious and superior sexual connection with the woman. But I was there first, darling, he thought, and I was there when it was beautiful and Harrison was fresh and sweet. She had picked up the child and was dragging the clothes basket towards the house.

He jumped from the rock and began to walk back towards the town.

Children. What about children? Sometimes he wanted them. Teaching them wasn't close enough. Did he want to mother a child? He remembered a strange night when he had gone to bed with Terri and she had wanted a baby. They talked about her and Mervyn and him bringing the baby up together. He'd loved the fantasy. Mervyn would kill him if he found him thinking like that. "Let those thoughts loose, sweet, and God knows where you'll end up—in the clinic at Rozelle—and hospital visiting is such a bore." He smiled. For Mervyn certain thoughts were taboo.

He wondered if Mervyn could really control his mind as well as that.

Mervyn had bought him a Siamese cat. "You need a family to look after," Mervyn had said. He'd bought himself an alley cat to prevent the Siamese cat from becoming snobbish and spoiled. He wanted to see Marlon, the Siamese cat. He missed Marlon. He wanted to stroke him and have him give back a purring warmth. God he needed that purring warmth all of a sudden. He preferred Marlon to James Dean. James Dean whined and had no pride. Like all alley cats. Like alley boys, too.

Perhaps he was ready for a Big Affair. With Mervyn? They hadn't talked *that* way. But perhaps it was getting to be *that* way.

For Christ's sake why was he going in for the introspection bit? Why didn't he just let it all happen—if it was going to happen? Why did he pester himself all the time? Why didn't he leave himself alone—stop picking at his mental nose? It was the damn homecoming, of course. But even at other times he was always picking at himself. As if to see if he would fall to pieces when prodded. Why did he bother? Everything was OK. He was a bloody good teacher. He had Mervyn, he had other friends, he had the garden, and his colonial cedar furniture. And they were always doing things.

Everything was OK. Everything was going fine. He walked up the curved green cement drive to his home. He hoped that his father would have lunched and gone to bowls.

He went inside. His father was still eating. His mother had waited for him.

"What did you do, dear?" his mother asked, putting his lunch in front of him.

"Walked about—up the street—up to the bush."

"See anyone you knew?"

"Only Harrison and a couple of others—from a distance."

"He's married with four children."

"So he told me."
"What did you do today?" asked his father, putting the newspaper aside with effort.
"Bernard has just been telling you," his mother said before he could reply, "if you'd only listen."
"You didn't come into the store—should see the extensions," his father said.
"I went up the street and looked around the new Commission houses," he answered his father. They both knew he wouldn't go near the store.
"The town's growing," his mother said. His father began to read the newspapers sideways.
He ate his lunch.
"Something wrong, Bernard?" his mother asked.
"No, just thinking," he said. "Beautiful salmon."
"You seemed quiet all of a sudden," his mother said.

HE WOULD HAVE liked to think that his visit home resolved something or other. But that was Young Thinking—to want to resolve everything simply by doing something dramatic. And really that hadn't been the reason for going home. Perhaps it had confirmed something about himself or his parents or something or something.
Mervyn was at the platform exit. "Oh come let us adore him! Really!"
Mervyn took the bags.
"How were the mater and pater?"
"Oh, you know . . . "
"Well, you've done the Right Thing—now you needn't bother till Christmas."
"I really don't think I could bear to go down again. There's *nothing*. And Mother comes to the city fairly often."
They walked to the taxi rank.
"How are Marlon and James Dean?"
"Marlon's been restless and moody—missed you dreadfully. Kept prowling around looking for you in such a possessive way."

He smiled.

"And James Dean is very happy—hasn't missed a meal. Absolutely without any feelings."

"Alley boy." They laughed at their joke.

They waited for a cab.

"I met my first love again—after fifteen years—nineteen years."

"How devastating. I never think of you having a First Time."

"He's gross—and married with four children. Lives in a *Housing Commission* area."

"Of course."

"He's not camp. I mean, he's never been camp. It was just kids' stuff."

They got into the cab.

Any cabs in the vicinity of St Mary's Cathedral—a Father Henderson for Vaucluse—thank you one-oh-nine —he'll be outside the main entrance. Someone for O'Sullivan Street, Rose Bay . . .

The traffic and buildings of the city gently ingested him. Mervyn laid a hand on his. He let the city take him. Its browns, blacks, and greys dressed with the red-amber-green of traffic lights and the mechanical dance of purple and orange neon.

Apples and Babies

THE MURMURING DROWSINESS of sickness. Outside the obedient pump motor starting when the house tank fell below the level. The bang of the screen door of the kitchen. The dim hush of the sick room. The smell of sunlight in the sheets. The still orange juice beside the bed. The prim, beaded cover on the jug. A curtain. A curtain tickled by the wind.

Jimmy Chanter who sat on my shoulder and watched everything I did, saw that I was awake and said: "Yes, this is Dural not Kings Cross. Those are apple trees out there

—not people walking up and down."

"Thank you, Jimmy Chanter. I don't think I needed to be told."

I ran my hand up the back of my neck and felt the short hair.

"Your hair and beard were cut by a barber brought to the house by your father who said, 'You can take the bloody lot off if you want as long as you make him look like a man!'"

"Thank you, Jimmy Chanter, but I remember."

Sue-Anne came in. Miss Fashion 1965. But I had to admit she had style. She sat on my bed.

"How's my young beatnik brother today? Withdrawal symptoms? Need a fix?"

"You read too many American magazines. I'm almost better, thank you. I'm almost ready to start driving from one end of the continent to the other. Go man go. That's if I had a car. If I had the money for petrol. If I had a licence. If I really believed the car wouldn't break down. If I wanted to go."

"A lady friend of yours rang to say that she got your note and she would see you when you returned. She was sorry that you were ill and wanted to be with you but you would know how things were."

"Did she give her name?"

"Robyn. No surname. She asked for me. How many women do you have?"

"I told her to ask for you."

"That was wise. Mother would not have been impressed."

"What did you tell her?"

"I told her you were recovering and would probably be back in town within a week."

"Thanks, Sue."

"Any time. I'm just the switchgirl for your life."

"I'll buy you that white sports car for your birthday."

"I don't need it, thanks. My boyfriend has one."

"What's his name? I've lost track."

"You don't know him. I doubt whether your paths have

crossed. Anyhow, why didn't your lady friend look after you? Why did you have to come home to Mummy and Daddy and sister?"

"She's married."

"Oh, how sad. Why do you bother? What's the good of a woman who can't look after her man?"

"That's how it happens sometimes, sis."

"I'd make sure it happened otherwise."

"I wouldn't make the mistake of thinking I ran the world if I were you, sis."

"I run my world thank you brother and my name is Sue-Anne not 'sis'."

Jimmy Chanter told me that I was getting my old spirit back again.

"Thank you, Jimmy. I'm feeling better every second."

"Who are you speaking to?" Sue-Anne asked. "Please don't go insane. We couldn't take that as well. Physical illness is enough."

"I was talking to myself. I find it rewarding sometimes."

Then Sue stopped bantering and her face showed concern. She looked down at me. She kissed my forehead.

"Stay home this time. Stay and help Dad in the orchard. You know they think you're home to stay."

"I guessed they might."

I saw myself sitting in the sprung, metal seat of a Ferguson tractor, ploughing between the rows of trees down the slope of a hot hillside. Fowls. Sunsets like explosions. The rustle of leaves like a concert audience. The night-time sounds of insects drawing outlines around the silence.

I let my mind see back to my room at Darlinghurst Road, Kings Cross. One wall magenta. On another wall, a nude woman with a hairy fanny drawn in charcoal. Perry's work. The sink choked with dishes. The drain with a mouthful of slops. Dead matches. Unwashed milk bottles with sour milk slime. A litter of books lying raped with leaves open like legs. My nevermade bed. Sheets the colour of dim light. Motor cars and voices always outside, scribbling over the silence. The air always smelling second-hand. Robyn hysterical about her husband. Margot saying that I could sleep with her but never to become emotionally involved with her because she was going to live with Perry.

"Think about it, Danny. Think hard about it. You've had your fling. You worry Mum and Dad sick the way you live. You don't have to go back to work at Woolworths. There are other jobs. You don't have to go into commerce. Find out what it is you want to do. Work with Dad here until you have. It's pleasant out here."

Sue-Anne had style and she was bright too. If I wasn't her brother or if I was incestuous I'd be interested in her. But she'd never drink at the George so I'd never see her or meet her. There is something very attractive about girls like Sue. Perhaps I should change my habits. Perhaps I'm tired of the chaos. There's an orderliness and a calmness about these girls.

"There was a bucket of hair after the barber cut it."

"I guess there would be. It was pretty long."

"It was down to your shoulders. But I told Dad he was wrong to do it."

"I knew it was all gone when I felt the draught."

"Think about staying, Danny, won't you?"

"For you, sis, anything."

Jimmy Chanter said: "Of course you're not going to think about it. You'd be out of your mind if you did." I told him to go away because I was tired. I was tired. Sue left.

Drinking from beer bottles in grimy kitchens. Dancing to worn rock and roll records. Talking about authoritarianism and Zen and about Burroughs and Ginsberg. Sending up your friends, sending up yourself. Talking just beyond what you know. Always being tempted out just that little way further beyond your knowledge. Wading out in the beer. Always more books to read. Someone else to know about. Always another party. Always someone's affair finishing. Another person gone to North Ryde Psychiatric Centre. Another lesbian. Another pill. Another idea about going interstate. Another way of making an easy quid.

Another idea about going to the country and living like a primitive.

Sue came back into the room.

"I don't know whether you'll be interested but next Monday night I'm having a few of my friends home to listen to records. We'll have a few drinks. Only about eight of us. Before you say anything I know I'm square and my friends are probably even squarer. But you don't have to act. Be yourself but don't swear too much and don't get drunk."

"I'll upset them, Sue."

"Rubbish. You make me angry sometimes. You don't even know how my friends think or what they talk about or what they believe. You sit so high and mighty at Kings Cross thinking you know about everyone and everything. Well, you're wrong."

"Nonsense. I just don't think I'll mix. Remember that I came out of the same hole in the trunk of the tree as you. I went to a private school too. I know what they're like and I know what I'm like."

"That was four years ago when we were all kids."

She went from strong to soft.

"Come, Danny. Just have a few drinks and talk about jazz or something neutral. But come along. It'll do you good. You need to be up and talking with people instead of lying about being depressed and angry."

"I'm not lying about depressed and angry."

"The doctor said that you were mentally exhausted."

"Doctors think all oddballs are mentally ill."

"Will you come?"

"Yes, I'll come."

"Thanks, Danny. I know it'll do you good."

"I won't get on the pot and rape all your sweet virgin friends."

"Don't be so sure about the virgin part."

Sue straightened the bed clothes and left again.

"Well, I'm re-entering bourgeois society. Up with the squares! I may stay here, Jimmy. You'd have to go then. I may reform. I may find myself a sweet virgin and marry and raise kids and work on an orchard. Hard work. A few beers in the local pub to wash away the dust. A shower and clean clothes. A well-cooked dinner from an intelligent private school girl who can cook as well as read Proust in the French. Who keeps the house orderly and hygienic. Who looks pretty when she's pregnant. Who has grace and style and knows about the subtleties of sex."

"How can she be a virgin and know about sex?" asked Jimmy Chanter.

"From books, Jimmy, from books. Ain't you never heard of books?"

But Jimmy had a point.

"Well, perhaps not a virgin but nearly a virgin. She had an affair with an older man who taught her all the secrets of a woman's legs and all the secrets of her hands and her sensitive, soft, screaming body. And she will eat with me while we talk about the international crisis about Saul Bellow and "Catch 22" and the *New Yorker*. We will have a good red wine and a good white wine in our cellar. Afterwards we will watch a BBC documentary on television or listen to the Stones. Or we may twist. We may lie naked while we sip brandy and ice. The whole setting will be serenity and order. The performance will be beauty and sensuality and everything will be productive and creative —apples and babies. The theme will be apples and babies."

I WENT DOWNSTAIRS for Sue-Anne's social evening. I felt colourless. I felt anonymous. The thing I liked about scruffy gear was that it identified you. It let people know something about you right from the beginning. It was like a street sign—people didn't take the wrong turn with you. And it wasn't a mask like most clothes—it was a direct expression of yourself. My corduroys and shirt had been washed and ironed by my mother and without my beard and cropped hair I felt as anonymous as a prisoner in gaol.

I was bumptious at first until I realised it. I talked with a fellow who was farming a few acres up the road. He was about two years older than me and married. I told him that the bomb would be dropped on it all before five years was up. I said this to show him that this sweat and work were futile.

He shrugged and said: "They won't drop it, they'd be too scared. But if we all go up I suppose nothing matters."

"Why sweat it out? Why not enjoy yourself just in case?"

"I work on the assumption that it's not going to drop. Anyhow, I have fun." He was answering me without smiling. He left to pour himself a drink and did not return.

Then Sue came over and introduced a sweet, virginal-looking friend named Sonia.

"Can you read Proust in French?" I asked, and Jimmy Chanter chortled.

"No, I don't think I've even read him in English."

"You'd know if you read him," I said.

"I'm always dubious about books in translation," she said. "I feel that I'm getting a vague, second-hand idea of what the writer is saying. It's probably a silly attitude."

We talked about books and she'd read around.

"Have you read 'Love in Action' by Fernando Henriques?" I said, again feeling that I was being bumptious.

"No, I haven't read any sex since my mother gave me a book when I was fourteen. It told me nothing. But I guess you pick it up."

I laughed. "You pick it up?"

She blushed a little. "I mean we talk about it. I mean you don't have to go to Kings Cross to learn about sex. It's pretty widespread you know." She was back on her feet again after tripping.

"I didn't mean that. I think you're more likely to pick it up in Kings Cross than anywhere. There's too much suppression in square circles. It's all taboo."

"Square circles? How can you have square circles?" We laughed.

I suggested we twist. So we twisted. We had a few drinks and talked. Then Mum and Sue-Anne served some supper. Sausage rolls and frankfurts and savouries. I'd forgotten about supper at parties. It must have been years since I'd seen supper at parties. I guessed that Mum was around to see that we didn't have an orgy. Fat chance.

She looked at me searchingly. Probably to detect whether I'd been drinking heavily.

"You go to bed early, Daniel. You're still recovering you know."

I nodded at her.

I asked the sweet virgin if I could see her home. She said she would like that. I borrowed Sue's car after arguing about me not having a licence. But Sonia lived only a few miles along the road and Sue relented.

On the way home I asked Sonia what she wanted to do with her life.

"I suppose you want to marry and have five children—or how many the Queen has—and then fight your life out with a husband about how much you are spending and how the kids misbehave and why things aren't fixed around the house and why he doesn't come home straight after work and why he doesn't kiss you as much."

She laughed and Jimmy Chanter said: "Oh boy, you are a wit."

But I was talking that way as an act. It was the way we all talked. But I had in my mind the apples and babies theme and it was a glowing thing. It was talking to me and I was letting myself listen, for the first time.

"I wouldn't mind going overseas."

"Why?"

"To get away from my parents. See things. Do things."

"You can get away from them by leaving home and living in the city."

"I probably couldn't afford it."

"Yes, you could."

"My parents would be OK about me going overseas but they wouldn't like me living in the city on my own."

"Show some independence."

"I would if I thought it worth it. I suppose it is worth it. I need someone to encourage me. I want to be free but sometimes it takes more than I've got. It means upheaval and arguments and I like peace and quiet."

We drove on past orchards. I remembered the arguments my parents and I had when I left home. I remembered them coming to see me at my Kings Cross flat. The first and last time. I had been embarrassed and aggressive. But I had stood against them.

"What do you want to do?" she asked.

"I don't know. Read. I don't know."

"You just can't read all your life."

"I know. I work a little now and then. I want to find out a lot of things before I decide to do anything."

"Do you go to university?"

"No, but I might one day. But I suspect it's just a degree mill."

"Do you write or paint or something?"

"No. I argue a lot."

A fox ran across the road. We both said "Did you see the fox?" and then we laughed.

"I'd like to edit a magazine that tore everything to bits." The idea had just occurred to me.

"You'd have to be a journalist to do that, wouldn't you?"

"No. Anyone could do it if they had the money."

"You sound as if you are leading a free life. I envy you."

"It's all right. It's all right, I suppose. It's a bit slummy. Sometimes I think of it as a search."

"What for?"

"I don't know. Perhaps it will lead back to apples and babies."

"What do you mean?"

"I don't really know. You know what? Sometimes I don't like the way I'm living but I look round and I dislike every other way more. There's just nothing else."

We drove on.

"Sue said you'd been sick."

"Yes, I came home because I was sick."

"It must be dreadful to be sick and alone."

"I wasn't alone exactly. But my friends had to go to work

and I was broke and couldn't pay chemists and things."

I suggested to her that we go out somewhere the next week.

"Yes, I'd like to do that."

"Where'd you like to go? I'm broke as hell."

"I'll take you out. I'll pay. But you decide where we should go."

"I don't know what your tastes are. Mine are fairly rough."

"Take me to the George Hotel for some drinks. I've never been there. Sue says you go there a lot." Her suggestion made me feel tired.

"All right."

We kissed goodnight and like a schoolboy I went home.

She wants to go wild, I told Jimmy Chanter.

"Yes," he said. "You don't have to tell me. And you want to go quiet. Next thing she'll be growing her hair long, wearing jeans, a boy's shirt, no make-up or shoes. That'll be the end of your private school virgin wife."

"Sometimes I think I'd be happier if I was in the paddock of conventions, safely grazing."

"The cows that graze safely are milked or slaughtered," Jimmy said.

"I guess that's right."

I garaged the car and walked out to look over the hills. The moon was painting the apple trees.

"We must play things by ear, I suppose, Jimmy, follow the music. But it's hard when you hear two tunes."

"I suppose it is," said Jimmy.

"How will the sweet virgin go at the Royal George?"

"Who knows?" said Jimmy.

"Will she like my room?"

"Who knows?" said Jimmy.

Anderson's Story

HE AWOKE from his dreaming with two incompatible emotional aches. The first ache came from the dying-down flames of his dreaming which had been about Wesley and the second came from once again realising that Sally and he had separated seven months before.

It was not the first morning that he had awoken with the incompatible aches. But as he reached consciousness he knew that this morning their status and strengths were different. The Wesley ache was dominant. The Sally ache was quiet and minor. This was new.

He had broken agonisingly with Sally seven tough months ago and yet his dreams since then had been of Wesley. He rolled into his pillow. He was tired of trying to understand his feelings and his condition. The dreams—dreams of Wesley rejecting him, often cruelly and laughingly—were the reverse of reality. He had rejected her. Not cruelly, but perhaps harshly. But all rejection was harsh. That was more than two years ago. Since then he had married Sally and was separated from her. Wesley and their young affair had been submerged under the ecstatic marriage. It had become a bitter marriage only towards the end. Bitterness about Marjorie and about having children.

He peeled himself a banana from a bowl of fruit beside his bed. He placed the skin in the ash tray where it was seized by gray ash.

Wesley: young love. Sally: mature marriage. Both failed. He was now frightened by the residue from Wesley. It was an old wound which had begun to hurt again. It should have healed. There had been no doubt that the affair was finished for him at the time. He had run to Sally, leaving behind him the young, broken Wesley. But he had felt no guilt and he refused to accept the guilt that now came from his dreams about it. He had known when he left her that he had no other obligation than to follow his strong, growing love for Sally — the delight of two always justifies the misery of one. He'd been a little dishonest with Wesley and a little harshly honest at other times but mostly he'd been gentle—honest or dishonest. Wesley had subsided into misery which only weeks of quiet nursing by friends could dispel. From reports he'd heard she had one day picked flowers and then slowly re-engaged with life and moved determinedly into a frantic dissipation. He heard now that she laughed louder than ever before. People said she spoke louder and trampled down her shyness with beer and sarcasm. He had heard her described as "tough". He guessed this was the grownup Wesley.

He tried to recall the rage he felt when living with Wesley. The rage would come when she spoke naively or when she made some foolish, ignorant remark. She tried too hard, and unnecessarily, to compensate for her youth. So unlike Sally who had been perceptive and sophisticated. But he could now only tell himself that this rage had existed—he couldn't feel it anymore. He wondered what to do with this new feeling and urge towards Wesley. He saw her body—and more womanly than the older Sally. Her breasts more thrusting than Sally's. He tried but could not realise that two years ago he could feel nothing but tired distaste for Wesley's body.

He stretched out of the bed falling on his hands and knees to the floor. He knew then that he didn't have a hang-over.

He wanted Wesley physically. He wanted also to talk with her about how dull and dislocated he felt after the breakup of his marriage. These realisations came to him with the clarity of radio.

He picked up his towel with his teeth and dog-like crawled to the shower recess.

Perhaps most of Wesley's irritating naivete and her poses of authority would have gone with the two years. Yet he was sure that her basic feelings towards him couldn't have. She was evidently still unattached emotionally. At least her letters—the one or two he had received in the last year—and reports from people who had seen her in Melbourne were without reference to a shack-up or marriage.

In the shower he tried to look into himself. He closed his eyes, leaned against the shower wall on crossed arms and let the hot water fall on his neck. He wanted to see his feelings. He wanted to be clear. His mind darted at his feelings trying to hold them, trying to grab them, trying to look at them or their strength and their direction. Each time the feeling would slip away and he would be left with a searching, panting, nonplussed mind. Then he would relax and let his feelings creep back from their hiding place and again his mind would dart and grab. He took the fact of Sally and his separation and held it against his feelings. They didn't cringe or hurt. He took the idea of Wesley and held it against his feelings and felt their jelly-like movement towards her.

He soaped up and said that this was a symbolic shower—the shedding of old grimes and a return to the innocent clean anticipation of new love. Or was it renewed old love? He remembered beautiful things he had done with Wesley in the time they had together. Of wood gathering in cold paddocks in the country for the cracking wood fires and the dull, comfortable booziness, backed by Pacific jazz. He had given away rich things to go with Sally.

He celebrated his cleansed feelings with grapefruit juice. To not follow and explore his urgings towards Wesley would leave open for always the possibility that he had avoided the chance of regaining these rich things. Two years of new experience had ground their personalities and perhaps this grinding meant that they now fitted more smoothly together.

IT WASN'T UNTIL he'd booked the call to Melbourne that he met the idea that perhaps he was irrationally turning away from the emptiness of his present life and trying to go backwards to a happier point. But his mind pushed off the idea with tired exasperation and refused to listen to the doubting. Let circumstances make these kinds of decisions. Let events compute the answer.

"One-oh-one to cabinet thirteen."

"Wesley, this is Anderson."

She was cheerfully cool. He told her he was coming down that weekend.

She questioned him with a stiff emotional defensiveness.

"Let's say it's for old times' sake. I'm crapped off with Sydney," he told her.

"If you feel you really want to," she said. Her voice was tight but it was not closed.

"And how's your designing?" he said, not wanting to explore any further towards her emotionally until he was with her. When he replaced the telephone his palms were moist and the black handpiece carried a patch of it.

WHEN SHE MET HIM at the airport he could see by the way she looked at him and could tell by the light kiss she gave him and from her general questions about his work that she didn't want to talk about their relationship. That this was for her a closed subject. He could feel her shying away and feel the fear she was harbouring as she interpreted his quiet, intimate tone and his physical reaching out to her.

"Let's go to a pub where we can be alone and talk," he said.

"Wouldn't you rather go home, have a shower and meet some of the crowd?" she said.

"No, I want to talk with you." He took her hand and his grip was stronger than old times' sake. He felt more remote than he thought he would. He realised that part of this came from the clothes she had on, which were all new to him. She wore nothing from the time when they had been together. She wore clothes which others had seen, admired and perhaps bought for her. But that was to be expected.

He bought two middies and they sat and they looked at each other for a quiet second.

He took her hand across the table and said: "Let's try again, Wesley. Let's spend a lot of time together and see."

She slowly and definitely shook her head.

"But I think things would be different now. We had so much. We had such an accumulation of good things. We can start again now—on what we had and on what we can do now."

"No, Anderson."

"Yes. We can. Please, let's try."

"You haven't changed, nor have I."

"But I have, and so must you. The separation has changed us. Time has changed us. I can see everything perspectively now."

"No, Anderson."

"You could be turning away from the best thing in our lives. We had something. We can have it again."

"Are you sure that you're not just trying to come back to me because Sally has gone? I'm not sure and I don't think you are."

"I am. It was conclusive. Final. I know."

"It doesn't matter. I'm not willing to try again."

"Are you attached to someone? I should have asked."

"No. I'm not attached. Just casual friendships."

"Well, let's try, Wesley. Let's have courage."

"We've got sentimental memories, Anderson. I've got painful recollections as well—you haven't. I'm unwilling to involve myself again. I'm scared of involvement."

"But you can't go on being scared. You have to risk or you gain nothing. You'll freeze up. You'll dry up. You have to live fully and involve yourself. You have to risk pain for joy. But we can be sure now, Wesley, because we're not strangers going into a darkness. We know each other. We know ourselves."

"I'm sorry, Anderson, but I can't. I'm settled here. I have a pattern of living. I'm not joyous but nor am I miserable."

"But Wesley, you deserve joy. We all deserve joy."

They talked for an hour or so. Not only about their relationship. Once he wondered fleetingly if it was more the challenge of regaining her that moved him or whether he still had emotional propulsion to her. But he didn't have time to find out nor did he want to. They left the pub and went to her flat, a little full, but with her still saying no. She refused to believe he had changed. But for the affection they still felt they went to bed and made love with a blues record playing and while they made love she said suddenly, "Yes, let's try again."

Afterwards they lay on their backs away from each

other, sweating, and talked about where they would live and what suburb was best and whether they would be able to buy a Ford Thunderbird as they had planned to do before. He told her of his new stereophonic player and she talked of setting up her own shop. She told him of her new recipe for garlic prawns Spanish style, and how she would cook it for him.

Then he heard her voice change its sound and become seriously intimate. "Anderson?"

"Yes, darling. What?"

"As soon as we settle let's have a baby."

He rolled over to her and put his hand gently on her face and said: "Yes, let's do that." His mind was angrily straining against the idea but his deceit was perfect. Then the anger broke its restraint and he thought how impulsive and inappropriate it was for her to say that. To ask that. It was so irresponsible and badly timed. But he couldn't say this to her. He rolled away as soon as he could without offending her mood. But she persisted chasing emotions.

"I want to have a child more than I want anything," she said. "I'm not going to wait until we have money or until we've got a bigger flat or any other reason. I want us to have a baby."

He placed a false hand on her saying: "You're beautiful."

They lay quiet together.

They made love again. He hoped that his anger would scatter but with cold fear he found himself smelling her and finding it distasteful as he had done two years before. Smells from between her legs which from Sally had been sweet, were from Wesley sour. They were sour two years ago and they were still sour. And he found her backside smell ugly and he kept going while the realisation of the ugly sourness came to him like smoke from a dead fire.

They finished and he lay in sweat, cold and worried.

"We will have a baby, won't we," she asked drowsily.

He didn't answer but touched her hair. Behind the gentle touch was regret that he felt for the mistake of their coming together again. He knew his touch was ambiguous and she understood it as a touch of love and assent.

He felt overwhelmed by his mistake. He could already feel Wesley's pain and confusion for her.

He went to the bathroom, clicking the door behind him. Alone with drying stockings and hair shampoo and other bathroom signs of her, he shuddered.

When he had finished in the bathroom he knew that he would have to unclick the door and then face her and tell her that it was no good—them going on.

Dead

SHE WAS SAYING: "I stayed with her right to the end, Mr Teller. It was pitiful—her retching and spewing. Nothing we could do for her. Just stand and watch. And then she died. Just like that."

Mrs Curry stood with the ten dollars, my rent, in her hand and told the story of her mother's death. Like telling about a film she'd seen. I stood with my sweating hand on the door of my flat looking at her through the hot dimness of the hall.

"She was terrible good to us while she was alive. She never had much but what she had she shared. And I can say I always treated my mother right, Mr Teller, I don't think anyone can say I wasn't a good daughter."

. . . and I was thinking about how my wife had left me yesterday, but not feeling love for her but not wanting her gone. And after three years of being together it was a grief not to have her with me. It had either knocked my heart unconscious or dead. So I was telling myself my own sad story and not wanting Mrs Curry's sad story. But I knew that I had to find something to say to fill the polite pauses in her description of the death, and I thought of saying we are a mixture of living and dying, even those of us who are walking around, but instead . . .

"I liked your mother very much, Mrs Curry," I said. "I

liked her very well."

"You know, Mr Teller," she said, "I still go to call out goodbye to Mum when I go to work. I have to catch hold of myself and say 'she's gone.' Well, she's in peace now, poor soul. I'll send down your receipt with Judy." Then she faded down the hall where it was dimmer and went in a door which was the boundary of her living and which kept her protected from the world, a garden of plastic flowers and an aviary of china birds.

Mrs Curry's mother had died in a room on the second floor, and now her niece Jill had moved in this morning. She had also told me that the owners had put up the rent, because Jill wasn't a pensioner like her mother. Mrs Curry collected the rent for the owners. She said that they couldn't wait ten minutes before they thought about putting the rent up. I had wondered how Jill liked sleeping in a death bed.

. . . on my bed I thought I knew that I had wanted Terri to leave me, but I had wanted her to stay with me too. I suppose I wanted the impossible—her staying with me until I got used to her not being with me. The upheaval and the change seemed huge and I was scared of it and scared of loneliness. My brain was gasping at it. I wanted to be salved by Elizabeth who was not free to live with me and salve me. Another thing was gritty in my stomach—I had not been completely honest with Terri. I had been a little honest with her after she had prised it from me with her terrible sadness, seeming to stab her heart with details of the affairs . . .

Then I heard Jill bumping bags on the stairs as she moved from one room to the other and I heard Judy, Mrs Curry's twelve-year-old daughter, as she helped Jill. Judy was the daughter, I guessed, of Mrs Curry's casual husband who came Saturdays to mend shoes in the sun on the brick backyard of our Surry Hills dwelling. He wasn't around much except for that. The shoes were a problem because Judy was learning to dance. She practised for hours on the bricks of the backyard to an audience of Jack Rusty, retired bookmaker and fellow tenant, a camphor laurel tree, and a furniture factory. She wanted to be a ballerina. Singing to herself, eyes closed, high on her toes, arms floating, she would whirl past the bottle stacks and lavatory, past Jack Rusty, the tree and the factory. Entranced. Now and then I I would watch her surreptitiously from my window. She looked sometimes like a candle flame in the backyard. And I would see Teddy Jefferey watching with a smile from his window in the jumbled tenement opposite. They said he was dying of cancer of the bowels and he didn't smile or grin much. Sometimes while Judy danced, Jack Rusty would cry out: "That's the girl, keep it up and one day we'll all start dancing—every-bloody-one of us." But I would wonder if the Mrs Curry who struggled to pay for the dancing lessons from her machinist's pay would be killed by the Mrs Curry who thought Judy was now too old to dance. But I didn't wonder today.

. . . today my eyes ached with a picture of yesterday when Terri had packed her bags with the anger of rejection and left. Yesterday—a hot summer's day of living. I cried for about ten minutes after she left. I cried heavily while she was in the room packing. And then looking at her packing her bags I had wanted to make love to her because I noticed her shape and movement again . . .

As I lay on my bed Judy's radio-singer voice rubbed against my window and I listened for the soft scrape of her shoes. All around me seemed to be this movement—shifting rooms, door banging, asking of questions up the stairs, cars going by in the street, hawking and coughing, Judy dancing in the backyard. The movement of my own life. Working-class girls wanted to be ballerinas and rich girls wanted to work in hotel bars. I wanted to lie on my back and think over every incident of my life with Terri. John Teller's life with Terri McDowell.

. . . deado. Terri and I were definitely deado. Finished. Our parting had been sure to happen. But now it had happened and I had Elizabeth, I was not as sure about it all —just a little unsure—at the heart of me. I was cold because I didn't know how Elizabeth and I would live it out together every day. And what if she didn't leave her husband? And what then?

But all our moaning, our dancing, our singing and the ticking of the clock were broken into by the ugly calling-voice of Mrs Curry. She was calling: "Ju-dee, Ju-dee, you come up here this very minute and stop dancing in your good shoes." It broke in on me.

Tell her to go to buggery, Judy, I said to the ceiling, because you won't dance when you've been chewed and spat out like your mother. You'll be deado.

Judy told her mother that she'd come but began to dance again, back to her dreams. Mrs Curry's yelling came again, tearing through the walls of my flat and down the brick backyard like a wind. It made me roll on the bed.

"You come here when I tell you, Judy."

You go there when you're finished, Judy, I said, but the words were too feeble to go very far from my lips.

A door slammed and Judy danced up the stairs to her mother's command, singing "The Blue Bird of Happiness." And the yelling started again.

"You don't love your mother, Judy. You're disobedient and cruel and you never do what I say. You spend all your time dancing. If only you knew how I slaved for you. You're ungrateful. You're an ungrateful wretch. You don't love me like I loved my mother—you're not like us. You're bad. Why don't you do what I say when I ask you? You don't love me, that's why. You don't love me, do you? Do you? Do you? Answer me, Judy." Judy was howling. "Answer me, Judy."

I rolled off my bed.

"Answer me, Judy," she screamed.

I opened the door through which I paid my rent and I yelled with all my force:

Shut
up
for
God's sake!

Along the dim hallway it bellowed but I felt that as soon

as the yell reached the part I couldn't see it would stop. I tiredly closed the door. The house was standing quiet.

The ticking of the clock came back and then faint, vague noises of the traffic on the street, and then I could hear Mr Rusty pottering around in his cluttered kitchen. But most of what came back was silence and I lay again on my bed saying in my mind: "Deado. Terri and I are deado. Mrs Curry is deado. But you dance, Judy, dance and maybe we will all get up and dance away."

Futility and Other Animals

SHE SAW IT for the first time when they were unpacking at the cabin in the isolated gorge country, and she said: "Why do you have a gun, Daddy?"

"For the security that might be in it." . . . Was it wrong to talk about security and insecurity with an eight-year-old? "Insecurity" is what you'll call it, he thought, when you are thirty-four and compulsively hiding your head under the blankets of your bed during an emotional gust. Probably all you feel now is that Mummy and Daddy don't love you enough, which isn't really true . . .

"But why, Daddy?"

"The gun? I've told you. It is a comfort to me like your old dolly is to you. See, if any wild animals come to the door I'll point the gun at them and they'll go away."

"Are there wild animals around?"

HE REMEMBERED a pot-high talk over a fire on a beach where he and Jimmy had slept for three nights, escaping the city's emotional magnetic field which had pushed and pulled both of them.

"Having a gun is political, Jimmy."

"But what about your non-violence and all that? Where does that all fit in?"

"Having a gun isn't being militaristic or aggressive. Or

being a thug. Having a gun is like having a vote. Or a say in things. A vote is for times of social stability and a gun for times of social disruption or upheaval. A man defends himself with an argument when confronted with an argument and with a gun when confronted with a gun." He said it like a part in a play.

And for a moment the pot made him feel the gathering of dark, dangerous times and upheaval and chaos and shooting. He could hear the shooting. Then dissolving into a drifting calm.

"With a single shot .22? Ho Ho Ho Ho," Jimmy said.

He heard the Ho Ho Ho Ho of Jimmy and smiled and loved him and giggled.

"A shot . . . single 22," he thought. "I was nearly shot single at 22."

HE HAD FOUND the note after coming from having lessons on the harp from Waterhouse. His usual Wednesday night lesson with Waterhouse. How had he come to want to learn the harp? He had tried but never mastered it. Worse, he had never extracted any sense of beauty or skill from it.

The note had read: "My dear, dear Perry, I was going to wait to tell you and then couldn't. I have gone over it in my mind for weeks and hidden it from you and feel so guilty. But I can't face you—not after how beautiful it has been now for eight months and not after how much it has meant for both of us. Anyhow, what it has meant for me. That sounds corny. And this note is all disjointed but so am I. Parting isn't everything and what we've got from living together is good in itself and lasts beyond us. As you will know, I've gone to live with Daniel. I didn't 'get over it' as you said I would. I'm desperately in love with him. I love you—but in a different way. Leave me for a while and then I will be able to talk to you about it all. Oh, my sweet. If only it could have gone on truly, but it's ending without becoming stale and that's good. Margot."

He had thought about this happening. But having thought about it in no way whatsoever helped him take the emotional pain which stormed him. He lay on the bed. Cried. Searched for sleeping pills to kill himself but found only three. Saw her toothbrush in the bathroom as though she was still with him. Lay thinking over the times together—the first time they had acted together, their trip in the canoes. His mind stabbed away with memories. He took the pills to stop that.

In the savagely lonely morning he tried not to wake. He wanted to crawl back to sleep but his body wouldn't take any more.

He rang Daniel's room and Daniel said he thought that Margot didn't feel like talking to him.

"Well, I bloody well want to speak to her so for Christ's sake put her on or I'll come around there and smash your fucking door down."

Margot cryingly confirmed all that was in the note and he cryingly reiterated his love. Oh, his love.

He had gone then to a sports goods store and bought the first rifle shown him by the assistant who wanted to talk of range and sighting. Who was nonplussed because sales talk wasn't necessary. Who wrapped the rifle so carefully with a packet of .22 bullets.

He had driven tear-blinded back to the flat. Carrying the parcel, he had been aware of the weight and balance of the rifle. The first awareness that morning of a thing outside himself.

In his flat he found Marylou.

"Margot phoned me last night and told me about it. She said I might be able to help. She's distressed about it happening this way." Marylou suggested getting drunk.

Before Margot, he had had an affair with Marylou and had been with her once or twice while living with Margot. Margot didn't know that. Oddly enough she had been a sweet, close friend to them both.

He had even laughed on that picnic. He got drunk, took some tranquilisers and passed out in the car while Marylou drove him to her flat where he lived for a month or so. The rifle lay unopened on his bed for that month or so. He had been aware of it while getting his clothes and stuff for his stay with Marylou. He had thought of it being there for when the pain came back beyond his endurance.

"DADDY, I asked you if there were wild animals here. *Talk to me.*"

"Yes, darling, there are wild animals down in the gorge but they won't hurt us as long as we have the gun."

"But what if they come in the middle of the night while we are asleep?"

HE HAD MARRIED Robyn and taken on the role of father of her child. She had found the rifle in his flat shortly after she had moved in.

"When did you get this, Perry? What in heavens is it for?"

He had forgotten about the rifle.

"A man should be able to feed his family—should be able to hunt. It's basic, primitive—good. It's fashionable to be primitive, you know."

"Yes, I must say that a rifle is very primitive. Tell me. That's not the reason. Tell me."

"It is. We face extinction unless we know how to preserve ourselves in a primitive environment. We're forgetting all the old skills and crafts but if we have to go bush to avoid the bomb or invasion or something we'll need them."

She hadn't believed him and kept asking.

He'd told her, feeling that it was probably necessary for the openness of their marriage.

"I bought the gun to shoot myself," he said. "I had a broken heart."

When they had talked away the incident and Robyn had digested this new thing about him, she had said: "Well, you're not ever going to be heart-broken again, my love, so why not get rid of it? Guns scare me."

He had said he would, but had not intended to and did not.

CHRIS HAD GONE to the cliff edge and was looking into the gorge for wild animals, bending, hands on knees.

"You be careful, Chris."

THERE HAD BEEN a time before his marriage when he had lost his way psychologically. When he had been swept with futility. Where it came from he did not know. From the gorge? He had walked out on a minor role at the Royal. He had stopped drinking at Watsons. He lay staring at the river. Sleeping fifteen hours a day. Saying what does it all matter?

He had loaded the rifle one day in the time of his deepest angst. The only time it had been loaded since its purchase. He had looked down the barrel. His patient servant. He had ejected the cartridge. Reloaded, ejected, reloaded, ejected. The cartridges spun across the room from the kick of the extractor. He had lazily symbolised it: saying, like human beings who fire their lives and are then ejected. Something like that.

The futility or angst or whatever it was at that time had not gone far away. It had come back, making him stumble after two years of marriage. Robyn had tried to help but he had been alone in a mental pit. He felt those around him looking sympathetically down at him, unable to help him rise. He wondered if he would ever fall down again, and if so, whether he would rise up. Robyn had thought that it meant he didn't love her or Chris. "If you loved you would not find life to be futile." But in time he had convinced her otherwise. He did not know if this had been honest. Futility came from a life which was ungratified. At these times especially, but at other times too, Margot was alive in his mind. It was that word love which he thought he should look at again soon. Futility was a wild animal all right, and the gun was a way of scaring it. It could be a way of killing it for all time. Perhaps it was best when used only to frighten the animal away.

"I SAID, WHAT if they come while we are all asleep?"

"Well, Chris, if they come in the middle of the night I will hear them because they make such a frightful noise and I will get up and frighten them away.

"But what if you're not here."

"But I will be here."

He gave Chris a lantern to carry into the cabin and he carried the rifle and the portagas stove.

The Second Story of Nature

SHE HAD BEGUN love-making with a passionate relief. It had been held off because of the visitors. Now the others had left, including Anne, his girlfriend from years ago. As the door closed they locked together, the cigarette smoke was still scattering and the beer dregs were not yet flat.

Standing, they kissed into each other, burning brightly with the sexuality of the beginning but eager with physical impatience—the physical impatience which would eventually swing them past completion, leaving the pleasure behind, to be contemplated for the short while and then forgotten. Their urgings took them further on. They leapt the forced pauses—the pause between standing embraced and moving to a lying embrace—the pause after rolling while they kicked off their shoes—the pause after intertwining, to pull off their clothes.

Their skins seemed to adhere where they touched. Their feet frictioned fire into each other. Their hands inflamed their hair. Their pushing stomachs and then the joining.

On and off during the time that they moved away from the closed door and towards the open bed, she was aware that she could become pregnant. She had not begun taking her pills that month and he didn't know. He would assume that she was. It wasn't till soon after he had entered her that she told him, finding strangely that she herself did not care and that she wanted him also not to care. He smiled and did not falter and went on, probably not from decision, she thought, but from the irresistibility of arousal.

This was the first time like this. She had furiously cared at all times before this and had never taken a risk—not for years—no, not ever. The problem flickered around outside her mind, just outside her concern. She saw that it was kept away from her by the heat of a kind of pleasure and the pleasure was that of feeling unconstrained. She was partly able to marvel at it as it happened and it was as though she was no longer drugged down or as though her legs were no longer tied. It was, she struggled to believe, a foolish, foolish reaction. But she was overcome by it and could not move to stop it. She was overcome by it and the loving. All her thoughts then, on this and her feelings about it melted into her immense feeling for Roger, laying her wide open and then closing her around him with the thudding and the burning and then the hot stillness.

They lay there, he looking away and slightly out of breath. She lay there, internally drenched. He dribbled slightly from his mouth, bodily slack. Her foot was caught in a twist of the blanket. She eased herself free and soundlessly scrabbled for cigarettes on the table beside the bed. And so it was a bed. And so it was a table. And then the room and the house were there.

"Want one?"

"No. Not yet."

She heard a woman's voice some distance away outside say: "No, it was the twenty-fifth." Somewhere she heard a toilet flush and a dog yelp. She moved her legs and it was moist and cold between them. But there was some warmth there with it. Like the lick of a dog. Uh uh, bestiality. He rolled off and away. He scratched his head and then his balls and said: "Oh, bloody beautiful girl."

She kissed his tit and said: "Yes?"

The interchange went nowhere into a silence and then she said: "Fucking is all now."

She moved her leg and pulled up the blanket because she was cool. He didn't want blanket because he was hot.

Incompatibility. Incompatible bastard. Bastardbility. "You are sometimes incompatible," she said tiredly, smiling.

"*We* are—you have to have a *we* to have incompatibility." He licked her navel under the blanket and inside her there was a stirring again like a whirl in her. A very little whirl.

"So, no pills," he said.

"I was going to tell you. I was going to stop for a month or so. They say to. The doctor said to. But I didn't tell you, didn't get around to it. It's kind of late. We should have done something."

He smiled at the ceiling and did not say anything.

"You mad at me?" she asked.

He shook his head and kissed her.

"It was odd," he said. And then added: "It was a kick."

"Yes," she said, thinking. "It *was* a kick."

"At least you are being very *was* about it."

"It has to be a *was* thing," she said, without much force.

They lay. She smoked.

Inside herself she began a rationality dialogue . . .

Women are freer now because they control contraception and it is premeditated contraception and they can be free of the fear of pregnancy and unhampered by devices and totally relaxed about it, but it means a daily sexual routine, a medical regimen, and it's a policing of the body and now suddenly I've broken the regimen and lost the freedom and am exposed to pregnancy and I feel a new freedom, a new free feeling, and it comes from being exposed to pregnancy and giving up control of my body and becoming reliant on a man to care for me, to be my . . . hunter and my soldier . . .

Mentally she slapped herself, shocked at the words which had come from her . . .

Irrational and mawkish and sickening. I am still for free loving and against conventional marriage and remain firmly so, and yet I see an involved relationship and its mutual dependence and I am not frightened. I may want other lovers but other lovers would be for passing pleasure and not for sharing of the dependence—and I think perhaps I'm just saying that, and will not want other lovers at all. The mutual dependence and that kind of relationship is a track down which only two can walk comfortably. I was different years ago. With Hugo. What would poor Hugo say about me now? Poor, emotionally deaf Hugo, grabbing when he should have been feeling, poking when he should have been touching . . .

"We're a bit neurotic," she said.

"More than a bit," he mumbled.

"Will we always be?"

He didn't answer.

"Perhaps our way of life is a sort of group therapy," she said.

"It probably makes us worse—sometimes."

"We couldn't be much bloody worse," she said, trying to make her cigarette smoke reach the ceiling.

"It's the nine-to-five people in the suburbs who are the happy ones," he said.

"What makes you say that?" Her sentence jumped from her mouth and stood astride his statement. What he had said was something that she was frightened was true. She had met it before and had not dealt with it. It was something she had put away.

"What they want and the way they live fits together. No conflicts. It all fits with the way they were brought up. They don't kick against it and it doesn't kick against them," he breathed out.

It was a long thing for him to say.

"But us," he said. "Sometimes we're arrogant and sometimes we're lost."

"You're oh-so-wise all of a sudden."

"Instead of emotional security we have only theories," he said, making a movement with his mouth in appreciation of his own succinctness. On the wall he drew with his finger an invisible picture of them both.

"But we have good times," she said.

"Yes."

"And we could have children and family and do good work and have a free sort of life as well?"

"The children would be sick, too."

"But they'd have their good times, too," she said.

They lay side by side, fingers touching. She smelt and liked the dry-cleaning of the blanket which had yesterday come back from the laundry, cleaned after two years of use. She thought how she was comforted by the blanket and how warm it was, and how woolly, thick and clean.

"Anyhow, what's this about having children?" he asked.

Was it a neutral enquiry or was it cautious?

"Nothing," she said, sensing that this was untrue . . .

Sometimes I feel desperately isolated, sometimes I feel inadequate and failed. Perhaps I should have married and had children. Sometimes I feel that by going to university and becoming a lecturer I have wasted my life and avoided the real living. Avoided fulfilment. Sometimes I plunge into these feelings and they do not go for sometime. But I would have simply been running away from demanding life to the hideaway of marriage where I would have been unchallenged and unthreatened. But I do not have a brilliant mind. I have not saved money and have no beautiful possessions and I move restlessly from flat to flat. I sometimes feel that I have wasted time, for all I have done. I am growing old. Sometimes I don't feel these things but feel elated and glad and I observe and listen and am breathlessly interested in living and painfully absorbed and I do feel acute enthusiasm and I am not preoccupied then with my feelings of mediocrity and misdirection I have ideas and I see things clearly and see people perceptively and am out of myself. *And then I feel other times drowningly involved with Roger and our living together. Sometimes we yell at each other. That was something I couldn't bear once because I wanted harmony. I didn't find harmony of that sort and I don't care much about it now. Why did I enjoy fucking without contraception? Why don't I care about it anymore?*

She softly began to quote to him: "I stand in the whirlpool and tell you I don't know and if I did know I would tell you and all I am doing now is to guess and I give you my guess for what it is worth as one man's guess. Yet I have worked out this guess for myself as nobody's yes-man and when it happens I no longer own the priceless little piece of territory under my own hat, so far gone that I can't even do my own guessing for myself, then I will know I am one of the unburied dead . . . "

"Who's that?"

She made to answer but he said: "No, let me guess. It's Sandburg, Sandburg the simpleton."

"You know because I always quote from Sandburg, and you can't abide him—incompatibility again."

"He's too simple."

"It's good to be offered simplicity now and then."

"Give me a cigarette."

She passed one to him.

"Well, what were you guessing about?" he asked, "And what is your guess?"

"About why it was so good."

"The fuck?"

"Yes—wasn't it good for you?"

He didn't answer immediately.

"I've already told you," he said. "It was a kick."

"A special kick?"

"Yes—a special kick."

"Why was it a kick?"

He shrugged.

"I know," she said defensively. "It's all sentimentality and emotional stuff from my upbringing coming up to the surface out of the murky depths of my unconscious. Just because for once I don't take the pill, I regress."

They lay in silence. She wanted him to contradict what she had said.

"I think it's more than that," she said after a while.

"What?"

"We are frustrated, repressed parents."

"Well," he said.

"We're at that age. Perhaps we are on the threshold of a

new experience."

"Mmmm," he said, softly, gently mocking.

"Do you ever feel like being a father?" she said, clambering atop of him, pinning his arms to the bed. "Answer me," she said in a loud tough voice. "Do you want a baby?" She watched his eyes and mouth and then yelled victoriously: "You do—you want a baby, I can tell. The bum artist wants to be a daddy," she gave a rebel yell.

"All right," he said, "don't get excited. I sometimes fancy myself as a daddy—but it's only fancy."

"It might be in my belly now—that fancy."

"That was a bit unplanned."

"You never told me you wanted children."

"You never really indicated an interest in the subject. On the contrary, it seemed to be very much out."

"That," she said, laughing at herself, "was yesterday."

She sat on his chest, thinking. "My baby?" she asked.

"Who else?"

She bent down and affectionately rested her head for a few seconds on his chest. Then she rolled off him, concealing her fast breathing.

"We're too selfish to have children," she said, without endorsing her words. She was excited.

"Perhaps we're too childish to have children."

"And we have other plans."

"Do you fancy yourself as a mummy?"

"Only now, for the first time," she said. "First time in my life." Then: "Perhaps it's a passing mood," she added.

She watched flashes of their life, with its boredom and its drinking and their tense friends and she wondered if she was changing. It was not a really representative set of impressions. She tried to see another life but no other offered. "Perhaps we could live in suburbia," she said. "It'd be unneurotic." She didn't believe it.

"You don't throw it like that—and who wants to? This is our way."

He was being certain. He was so often noncommittal.

"Yes, I know. We-should-learn-to-live-the-imperfect-life-graciously-as-is-our-lot." She said it with tired acceptance.

He didn't comment but lying face down on the bed said in a muffled voice: "So you want to have babies," and laughed into the pillow.

She pouted and moved away, interrupted in her mood, offended by his flippancy and his accuracy. He looked up and grinned at her pique. He tickled her and she screamed first with irritation but collapsing into the pleasure of it. They rolled, giggled and fought.

They lay panting.

Getting her breath: "Well," she said, "I think having kids is a good idea. Women can keep their freedom and still have kids. So there."

"What an interesting change of position," he said. "I begin to suspect you've been corrupted, Cindy. Catholics?"

She ignored him and said: "Why was it so good, Roger? I mean this time? Not that it isn't always superb."

He turned to the wall and with his finger traced a new picture of them both. "You're the one who reads all the books," he said.

"I guess they'd say that I was fulfilling my true biological function and conforming to the values of my upbringing and therefore felt totally free of guilt."

"Sounds very academically correct."

"It's sad."

"What's sad?"

"That what we believe seems to change our emotional life so little."

"As long as it makes some difference."

"It all sounds like surrender, doesn't it?"

"It's not only the squares who want to have children."

"Fucking without pills or anything must be different because of a lot of things. I mean it's alien to the sex act, isn't it? There's nothing intrinsically good about contraception. I mean, is there?"

"We talk about everything too much."

His old theme. "Pooh. I could say you draw things too much. It'd be just as stupid."

He smiled. It was an old argument.

"Are we still going to France?" she asked.

"Of course we're still going to France. We haven't had a baby yet, for God's sake."

He clutched her around the body and bit her back. And they made love again, rollingly, and softly, and quickly. She came up from it with a leg hanging over the edge of the bed, conscious that it was dark outside and that she could smell the cooking of cabbage drifting from some neighbouring kitchen.

Murmuringly she said: "Again—and you do it again. Now we will have two babies."

He grinned and stretched, clenching and unclenching his hand.

"You never do it twice," she said. "Not since Christmas and then it was the champagne—a champagne erection, that was."

"It's the new, hot, fertile you."

"I've never thought of myself as fertile."

"You have a fertile stench."

"Is that good?"

"Fine by me."

She lit a cigarette. He took it from her. She lit another.

"You know something, Roger," she said seriously. "I've never felt this emotional urge before in my life. Never. Not with Sean. Never with Hugo. On the contrary I was dead against it with him. Did I ever tell you about him and the pills?" She raised herself on her elbow. "He wanted children. Did I tell you about what he did?"

"You've told me about Hugo the hunter and Hugo the man who ate nuts and berries but never about Hugo the pill."

"He threw them away."

"The pills?"

"He wanted me to have children so he threw away the pills one day."

"What did you do?"

"I walked out."

"What was his problem?"

"He said that children were natural and the pills were unnatural and we were to have babies as they come—if we loved each other. I was only twenty."

"Catholic?"

"No, he was Lutheran—but an agnostic. Just wanted to have children all over the place."

"Very odd men you involve yourself with," he said, getting out of bed. "I'm going to have a leak."

She wandered back to the affair with Hugo, carefully uncovering memories left untouched for seven years . . . .

"I want children," he said loudly, gesticulating the expression So-What-the-hell's-wrong-with-that. "You must be out of your mind," she said. "Love goes bad between people when they don't want children," he said, "contraception is a rejection of children—a rejection of me as a father of your children. It's hesitancy." He talked quickly. She remained standing at the bathroom door, toothbrush in her hand. "But—I've got a year to go at uni. We've never even discussed it. You've never mentioned it. It's unbelievable." She was rigid with anger. "Love implies children," he said, buttressing his words with a heavy definiteness. "Children are the other part of the natural equation." "That's crap. Crap. What shit." "No, it's truth." "I don't give a damn about children. You threw away my pills. You authoritarian shit." She remembered other things he'd done. Theatre bookings without consultation. Things like that. "You didn't ask me whether you could use them. You didn't tell me you were using them. Who imposed on who?" he shouted. "For God's sake, only a fool wouldn't—you're—you're like all men. You think we can be used for your—fantasies." He didn't move his hands from the table where they lay palms down in front of him. As though he was about to rise. He began to colour. "So children are a fantasy. You're hung up—hung up on modern crap about independence. You think being independent means being neuter. You're hung

up Cindy." "You monster." "Having children means being a woman. That would scare the living shit out of you." "I don't want to be a woman," she yelled, sensing the bad tactics of the admission. "I mean, I don't want to be that sort of woman. Your sort of shithouse, servile woman."

She opened the window and hung out, her breasts pushed against the sill.

Shivering, Roger clambered back into bed.

"You're wet," she complained. "Don't men dry their penis?"

She stared at the backyards, at the corrugated iron bonnets on the backyard toilets with their ribald saw-tooth grins and the clothes lines like crazy cats-cradles.

"Hugo would like me now—steaming with fertility. Is that sexual? Does that sound sexy to you?"

"When I thought of you steaming with fertility it felt sexy. I felt pretty good when I held my cock just now – out pissing."

"Because of the babies and all?"

"Perhaps," he was uncomfortable about the admission and she noticed, and let it go.

"I told Hugo I didn't want to be a woman."

"What in God's sake did you want to be?" he asked with surprise.

"I wanted to be an intellectual with a vagina."

He guffawed and she blushed.

"Well, bugger me," he said. "Why don't you make some coffee, *woman.*"

"Is that a big male order?"

He gave her a loving push.

"But I've realised that we have to come to terms with our background and the way we've been raised," she continued with lament. "We're just not free."

"Make some coffee."

"You shut up." She lay back for a few seconds of protest and quiet sadness about what she'd said but this worked itself into a relief of self-recognition—something she was coming to accept. She rose and pulled on his duffle coat, freeing her long hair from under its collar, and brushing it a few times. She went barefoot to the kitchen. She sat on the table with feet on a chair as the water boiled, the coat hauled around her, too long at the sleeves and with shoulders which drooped down her arms. "I've been rescued from the sea and pulled aboard a ship and a sailor has given me his coat to keep me warm in the freezing Arctic night."

She was bodily alive. She pulled the coat apart and caressed her stomach with her hands down to her crotch and imagined a baby swelling her rounded, tight stomach. She caressed up to her breasts and handled the weight of them.

"I'm pregnant," she said impulsively at the bedroom—to try the sound and feel of the statement.

He made a snorting noise.

She put a Leadbelly record on the record player.

She wiped down the beer-puddled table.

She picked up the empty beer bottles which stood in groups on the floor, symbolising the drinking groups which had emptied them earlier.

Rooms seemed very empty after Sunday parties.

She tore March from the calendar, which was three days expired.

She put back the book "The Idiom of the People" and wondered who'd been looking at it.

She poured the boiling water onto the instant coffee and added three sugars. She felt feminine sometimes from doing things—even things as simple as that. Feminine. The word had once nauseated her. He did things for her—like unscrewing stuck lids—for all his bitching. But it was only a good feeling now and then. God protect her from being overwhelmed by it. It was a good feeling but it had dreadful, insidious dangers. It was a treacherous word. It could push you back into the pit.

She took him his coffee, carrying it as if it was full of dangers.

"What will we do the other times?" she asked.

He shrugged, sitting up to take his coffee.

"I suppose I'll have to get fitted with a diaphragm," she said. "I hate the thought." She sat hunched on the bed, pushing back the long sleeves of his heavy coat. "There's a strong smell of sperm about the bed," she sniffed. She felt secure and protected simply because she was wearing his coat. She scoffed. "I'm weakening," she thought.

"You could abstain," he said.

"Ho ho."

"You could have babies."

"We may even yet have babies, my dear, dear man." she said, sipping her coffee. "And what would you do, Roger, if I were?"

"What would *you* do?"

"I don't know what I would do. I'd probably . . . probably—have it." She moved her shoulders slightly as if in resignation, or perhaps, acceptance or perhaps uncertainty.

"Would you?" he asked.

"But I wouldn't get married. There's no reason for that," she said aggressively.

He said nothing.

"You haven't answered," she said.

"I'd probably want you to have it. In my present mood I wouldn't mind," he said, slurping.

She contemplated his answer with a beating stomach and then, twisting around, put down her coffee, and grabbed him, sinking down into him as though in warm mud.

"My fertile fuck," he said softly, holding her with one hand and his coffee with the other. "Watch out for the coffee."

"But what will we do? What are we going to do for the month or so—make a decision!" She demanded.

"Let's play sexual roulette for a month," he said lightly.

"It's immoral and irresponsible," she laughed.

"We've nothing to lose. We still go to France—might be three of us."

"It's irresponsible," she laughed. He put down his cup.

THE SEX THEY HAD that month was free and steaming, she thought, although she was less aware of any difference later in the month. Towards the end she remembered only now and then. She was sure that Roger responded to her vulnerability. She often made herself conscious of it, playing with fertility fantasy during the month. Roger said he sometimes remembered it and became excited by it.

At the end of the month she was not pregnant. She met her period with the same inevitabity as she would the end of a play, but it psychologically halted her for an instant—as if she'd expected never to see blood there again. Disappointment flashed and then was gone. The period burst her fantasy and switched her back to her former way of life. Perhaps there was relief there too. She revived and played with the idea of going to France.

Coming from the bathroom she said to him: "Well, now we can go to France." He didn't look up from the drawing board where he was working.

"We were always going to France," he said, head down.

"I'm not pregnant," she said. "That's what I meant."

He looked up and smiled at her. "Oh that." And went back to his work.

She stared at him.

"We really didn't have to have one and not the other," he said, not looking up. "We could have both."

She was surprised.

"I thought it would be easier to travel without a child," she said, finding herself unwillingly putting the tough line.

"Perhaps," he said, preoccupied with his drawing. "We might have them over there after we've been around."

He kept on working and she watched him, with some amazement.

She realized that it had happened, simply like that, and that they both now accepted the idea of children in their relationship and she had now no disappointment or relief about the month not yielding. She guessed that the idea of children would hang around with them now wherever they were.

The Third Story of Nature

SHE SAT CROSS-LEGGED on the bed, her thighs cradling the weight of her pregnancy. She had wanted to feel the weight from the day she knew she was pregnant. She'd wanted to feel pregnant. She did not have to imagine now.

"You'll have to keep the place cleaner than this when baby comes," said her mother, moving outside with a five-pin cluster of beer bottles, holding them away from her in a gesture of dissociation.

"You must admit that I've improved," she said, humoring her mother.

She watched her mother wipe her hands on the apron as she came inside. She watched her mother come across to her and she felt the hand on her face.

"You must look after yourself, Cindy. It's a critical time."

"Mother, I'm twenty-six."

"In some ways you're still a child. Now promise your poor old mother that you'll be good and keep the flat clean."

She almost nodded but her mother moved away from the uncertainty of her answer. Pulling on her rubber gloves her mother began to clean the bath with a righteous vigour.

"You could come home until after baby arrives. Father would love to have you home," her mother called, her voice hollowed by the resonance of the bath.

"That's out of the question."

Her mother refused to concede Roger the rights of a husband. In his casual way Roger didn't claim them and in the formal sense he wasn't a husband. What rights? The old trap again. The trap of looking for established patterns of rights and explanations. Established patterns were used by people whose relationships were too weak to generate their own living patterns. Or perhaps all human relationships were too weak to do this? Did they all require social patterns? Was it childish arrogance to think otherwise?

Were social patterns congealed wisdom? Social patterns changed. And some people changed faster than social patterns. Some people were out of synchronisation. "Synchronise your watches."

"But sir, we have no watches." Were you in the vanguard or simply impatiently running on ahead—to find yourself without society—isolated and scared with other isolated and scared people?

"We just thought you might like to come home, dear," her mother said, her fangs retreating into a chatting mouth.

"Sara and I walked out of a film for the first time for years, the other day. Hopelessly silly thing it was. I'm afraid I don't understand modern films."

"What was the film?"

"A thing called 'Morgan'."

"Oh—I'd heard it was funny."

Roger had said it was funny and Ken had raved about it.

Of course, just because you were married did not mean that you weren't having a living relationship. But married people hampered themselves.

"Here, dear. Your eyes are younger than mine. What does it say on the label? Two tablespoons to the gallon?"

"Yes. Two tablespoons to the gallon. Warm water."

Relatives and acquaintances and society felt legally justified in applying all sorts of pressures to ensure that you conformed to their idea of marriage. And you tended to adopt their ideas from tiredness. Because she and Roger were not married their parents were generally wary and uncertain. They came to visit with a frightened curiosity which could change to blustering aggression. But these things didn't worry Roger. He didn't discuss them either. He lived simply by his personal tenets. She didn't have tenets. She wished she did. She had only tentative wild ideas to live by. Sometimes the ideas ran away from her.

"I'll do the toilet and then I must go."

"Don't bother, Mother. Leave it—please."

"You make a cup of tea. That would be something useful."

Her mother would clean the flat, arranging the books, dusting, organising the kitchen cupboards with clean newspaper, throwing away old food from the refrigerator. But she would not touch the bed. The bed was a symbol of her daughter's defection. Periodically her mother did this. She made these cleaning attempts to retrieve her from the degradation of her runaway disorganised life—tried to pull her back onto the middle-class boat. Her mother cleaned the flat regardless of its condition. And it was always hygienic even if it was sometimes disarranged. Her mother would also buy her clothing from David Jones—clothes which were to serve as a uniform and a correction to her daughter's deviant taste. She would clean the flat and ask her to come home.

She hauled herself from the bed and to the kitchen. I'm beginning to waddle, she thought.

"Next time I come I'll bring my new detergent. It's really excellent."

"Oh?"

"Father brought it from the factory. It's for industrial use. I use it around the house."

"Roger hates the smell of detergent."

"This has a lovely clean, strong smell."

Her mother's virtue for cleanliness had become a violent, acidic thing. She turned on the kitchen tap and let the harmless water run over her fingers. She filled the kettle. One day her mother would find a detergent which would keep all things permanently and deeply clean. Her mother would bring it to her and wash out her life and bathe her in it. From then on she would never be able to again feel dirty or have a sweating fuck. But at least the soles of her feet would not be gritty after walking from the bath to the bed. That would be something.

"You'll have to tell Roger to keep things clean. It's dreadfully important when you have a baby."

"He thinks we keep things too clean."

Once he had yelled at her: "Don't try to impose your Mother's sterilised existence on me."

"Yes, well, we both know how funny he is about some things."

The kitchen alliance. Her mother had in one sentence taken her into the female alliance against men—mother and daughter. The female superiority of "understanding" their men.

God knows she wanted it sometimes—not against men—but to be in female alliance. To rest upon the certainty of female knowledge. To understand by female intuition. To have a set of female tasks and female skills to handle them. But that female alliance belonged to the order and the cleanliness and stability of the home she had left. At times she wanted them too. A home unchanged and clean for forty years—changed only by accumulated decoration of the basic theme. Sometimes she fantasised that she would surrender back. Her mother did not know how close she came at times to crying "oh, Mother" and flying back into her arms. But she did not. Did her mother want her back—an adult child? Did she want back a wayward baby? She had no place back at home, except as a visitor and then as an uneasy one. Her "place" always kept, was a sepulchre for them to regret at, not a refuge for her to go back to. She was supposed by now, according to the rules, to be in her own home, working daily to imitate the cleanliness and order which becomes stability when it has been maintained for twenty-five—or how many years equalled stability? Even then perhaps it was threatened daily and one never knew when one had stability. Her mother lived in a threatened world of headlines and news flashes which said to her "morals are changing, prices rising, workmanship is poor, fashions are ridiculous, communists and trade unions run the country, community spirit is dead." Perhaps her mother feared daily that her prayers and her polishing and British troops would not be enough to hold back the seeping chaos. Perhaps she was nibbled by fear that others were not putting their rubbish in the Be Tidy bins—that others were not trying.

"Father's having trouble at the factory—unions again."

"What's the problem?"

"It's not the men—it's their leaders. The men are decent enough. It's the leaders who make the trouble. But for them there would be no strikes."

She could not reply. On subjects like this she choked with irritation. She didn't give a damn about trade unions but when her mother attacked them she was swept to their defence. She could feel her breathing break rhythm. Her mind fumbled.

"The cost of living is always rising," she said, ineffectually, moving a cup and saucer in a sort of physical twitch.

"They make it rise—they send the prices soaring," her mother said, looking for a broom behind the door. "You'd think they'd wake up and see that high wages make the prices rise."

"There should be price control."

"No dear," her mother used her condescending voice, kept for statements which she thought carried the wisdom of years, for eternal truths. "We had that during the war and it didn't make a scrap of difference. You have the black market then. Human nature can't be changed."

No matter how calm she tried to be her mother's tone and her arguments made her heated. She sweated in an impotent silence. Why did she bother? Was it that she felt herself attacked unjustly by her mother and therefore defended anyone attacked by her mother?

"Cindy, dear—I've been telling you all your life to heat the teapot before you make the tea. Sometimes I think you just do it to annoy."

"I don't think that in summer it makes much difference, Mother, I really don't."

"It's the only way to get a good hot cup of tea."

Her baby would be born into a time when granddaughters would not understand their grandmothers. Already mothers and daughters were having difficulty. Perhaps we were creating an orphan generation—no parents and no God. Where had she heard that—someone in the common room? She corrected herself. It was not the whole world that was alienated from its parents, only the teenagers and they for only a short time. They mostly fell back and went about imitating their parents. It was the intellectually rebellious and the neurotics who went on feeding and nursing their alienation—proceeding further in the direction away from their parents. But her daughter would be freer. Her daughter would be offered more alternatives and less censure. The following of strange paths would be easier for her and she would have a mother who—if she had not gone far along the strange paths—at least understood why some people did. Or did she understand? What was so great about nonconformity? What was so great about independence? What was so good about strange paths? Perhaps her daughter wanted a familiar path? But whatever, her daughter would not live with the emotionally gruelling voice which said "Do you really think you are doing a wise thing?" whenever she deviated from the normal. Again, perhaps this was a useful exercise. Perhaps there was value in living with a question like that. Her problem was that her judgements were hooked to values she no longer held. This was something she could help her own daughter with. The freedom to develop values suitable for her times and her personality. How for God's sake? How did one do that? She had been tormented about becoming a lecturer instead of marrying and setting up home. She had been tormented about her sexual behaviour. Worse, she had to pretend to herself that she had no conflicts. Middle-class girls make poor rebels.

"You don't seem very happy, dear. Was it something I said?"

Was it something she said!

"Oh, I'm fine. Just thinking."

"I hope you're not worrying."

"Oh, no."

Oh, no.

"You'd tell me. Wouldn't you?"

Tell you!

"I'm very well and everything is fine." She held back her

irritation and kissed her mother on the cheek.

They sat down with their cups of tea and her mother stirred hers too long.

"I don't want you worrying. Not at this time."

They chattered about her aunt and her brother. Her mother washed up the cups. Her mother talked about a road accident which had killed the son of one of her friends.

The road accident had become a folk drama for her mother—and perhaps a mortality play asking "Why do some of us have to die this way and why do some die so young?" The road accident was the unpredictable terror in an otherwise predictable society. Everyone had their accident and their escape from death. It was the idea of chaos again. The road accident had the music of chaos—the screech, the smash, the tinkle, the scream, the groan, the high pitch of stuck horn, the siren. The siren was the way we announced the conflict between order and disaster.

Her mother was now standing in the room, her hands on her aproned hips surveying the work she had done.

"If you do a little every day you can keep it clean. When baby comes you'll have other things to worry about too, you know."

The baby would bring chaos if you weren't careful, you know. If it was not fought with order and hygiene it would cause a life smash. Her mother often treated her as if she had been in a life accident. But she saw the threat of chaos too. Perhaps she would be dragged down into chaos by dirty nappies and crying in the night.

"Please think about what Father wrote to you. If only for baby's sake. The little mite should have the protection of marriage—even if you don't want it."

"What protection is that?"

"Legal protection. Just in case something happened."

"What legal protection?"

"Well dear, I don't like broaching these things but we have to be practical. What, for instance, if Roger left you? I'm not saying that he ever would—but there's nothing holding him, is there?"

Her mother had sat down beside her and had assumed a businesslike voice. A for-your-own-sake voice.

"There's me and baby. What more can there be?"

"But if you married him there would be a legal obligation for him to look after you both."

"I resent that. You shouldn't say that." She was calmer now but emotionally aroused. "For God's sake, laws don't hold people together. They might stay together in one house, technically, but who wants that? And who wants money that has to be forced out of someone you love?"

"Dear Cindy, you must be sensible. It's not only yourself anymore. There's another person to think of now."

"I am thinking of baby. I want a real relationship—not a legal document. I don't want to be able to say to baby: Look, Daddy's gone but we have this certificate and ten dollars a week from the court." Her agitation made her get up and without reason she washed her hands. But she still had mental confidence.

"It's much nicer to have things done properly." Her mother's voice changed, softened, and the fangs withdrew. There was a religious idea driving her mother too but this was not mentioned.

Her mother began rubbing at a stain on the kitchen wall.

Her mother's presence in the flat suddenly insulted her. She felt that she was being aggressed. Her mother was not offering assistance, not reaching out to her. She was manipulating her. She was trying to control her. Her values and aspirations were not being accepted—they were being attacked.

"I want you to leave, Mother."

It was sudden. She was suddenly cool.

Her mother stood shocked.

"I feel that you have come here to impose yourself. You don't like me. You don't like my way of life. And you interfere. I don't feel I can resist you any longer because I'm tired and weak. Please go."

"Cindy—I was trying to help you." Her mother put one hand on her. The other held a Wettex.

"Please go. I don't want to fight with you."

"We've never fought, Cindy dear. We've never."

"Please leave." Her voice slightly louder.

"You can't talk to me, your mother, like that." Her mother's voice became bitter and strong.

She went over and picked up her mother's coat and hat. She handed them to her.

"Get out."

"This is deeply, deeply hurtful to me," her mother said. Her voice lowered—a prelude to crying. Another way of manipulating.

She remained silent. She looked at her mother's face closely—for perhaps the first time. Saw the pores and saw the wrinkles and saw the shape. She saw it as a woman's face.

Her mother dabbed at her eyes, gathered herself, took off the apron. She came over to her and gave her a hard kiss.

"We'll think of you. You are not yourself. But when you want help come to us," her mother said, knifingly.

"Go, please."

Her mother left. She closed the door and bolted it. She felt freed. She trembled and agitation shook her. Today she had not been submissive. She listened to her mother clacking down the stairs. She thought of the hopelessly shattered links between the three generations which had been at afternoon tea.

She sat down shaking, but released. Roger would be home soon. Or would he? Would this be the night when he did not come home—the night he would be with some other girl? It would be only for a night or two—she was sure of that. Was she sure of that? He never had got off but the possibility was always there, built into the relationship. She needed Roger not to get off now, of all times. Her conventional breeding cried for conventional comfort. At least for a make-believe security. Sad she needed to make believe that she was as safe as her mother. She wanted to make believe. Even though Roger had given her the security of honesty and the implicit pledge to be the father of their child.

She sat in the middle-class clean flat and brushed her hair for Roger, still trembling. I am frightened, Mother, she thought, and I do fearfully wish there was a document which would guarantee love. And if you had asked one more time perhaps I would have gone home with you, Mother. But not after today.

Frank Moorhouse
The Americans, Baby

Meet Becker, the Coca Cola Kid, lost in Australia and longing for Atlanta . . .

Meet Dell, a country girl looking for excitement and love in the city . . .

And experience the exquisite embarrassments of the American Poet's visit . . .

Against a background of political activism and the Vietnam War, *The Americans, Baby* captures the lives of a generation in transition, a generation for whom 'liberation' and loosening political, social and sexual boundaries have brought both new freedoms and new uncertainties.

'a textbook of the times'
Donald Horne

'the best short stories we've had in Australia for a long time'
THE BULLETIN

'The most accomplished historian of conflagrations over the past twenty years . . . Thank goodness . . . for Frank Moorhouse'
TIMES LITERARY SUPPLEMENT

' . . . one of the most assured craftsmen and original writers of fiction in Australia today'
THE AUSTRALIAN

Frank Moorhouse
The Electrical Experience

'The Greeks believed there was a time in the past when things were easier. The scientifically minded person believes that there will be a time in the future when things will be easier'

from a speech by T. George McDowell

T. George McDowell believes in Getting the Job Done. A manufacturer of soft drinks on the south coast of New South Wales, he is a Rotarian, an apostle of Progress, of electricity, refrigeration and the wireless.

Of the generation born just after Federation, T. George McDowell sees himself as a bastion of quality, reason and stability in a world that is not changing for the better. His youngest daughter, Terri, seems determined to put his beliefs to the test . . .

'The material . . . is treated with the rueful truth of art'
THE NEW YORKER

' . . . a great writer who X-rays the Australian soul'
LE MONDE

Winner of the National Book Council Award for Fiction

Frank Moorhouse
Grand Days

One day in the nineteen-twenties on the train from Paris to Geneva Edith Campbell Berry meets Major Ambrose Westwood in the dining car, makes his acquaintance over a lunch of six courses, and allows him to kiss her on the lips.

Both are heading for Geneva to posts in the newly created League of Nations and this intimacy binds them together in a private and public journey.

In those grand, glorious days, nothing seems beyond the intelligence and administrative talents of the young diplomats of the League. The prevailing mood of exuberance carries over into the Geneva nights. Edith, beckoned on by Ambrose, ventures into the darker recesses of the times.

Moorhouse's dazzling evocation of a golden, all-but-lost era and the unforgettable central character of Edith make reading *Grand Days* a rare experience: it is vivid and wise, full of shocks of recognition and revelation. The final effect of the book is intoxicating and unplaceably original.

'Moorhouse has for a long time been one of the most original and professional of Australian writers in the world of literature in English. *Grand Days* is the summit of this achievement'
GEOFFREY DUTTON, AUSTRALIAN BOOK REVIEW

'Not only is the book intricately researched and convincing, it manages to be funny, scary and extremely sexy, mingling the comedy of petty diplomacy with the storm clouds heralding World War II and the thrilled but tangled eroticism of the time . . .Truly a grand book'
UK VOGUE

Frank Moorhouse
Loose Living

To learn my French, I attend the acclaimed Ecole Français for four to fourteen year olds, of which the Duc is the dubious patron . . . But unlike an Australian school you are not surrounded by hopeless drawings of houses with windows in the wrong places and endless smoke curling out of chimneys. The French children draw wine bottles and table settings. A typical playlunch at the school is a couple of quail in aspic and a tossed green salad, washed down with a small glass of vin ordinaire.

As Australia turns to Asia, Moorhouse's hero is permitted one last look at Europe.

Here are his dispatches home, detailing his arrival in the wondrously civilised world of France; his glittering life at the *château* with the Duc; his fall into disgrace at the Ecole des Beaux Arts Perdus; and his appointment as Gregarious Fellow at the Montaigne Clinic for Civilised Disorders, deep in the Pyrenees.

Loose Living is Moorehouse's third book of comic writing, and incisively dissects our contemporary New Sensitivities. It is his funniest and most provocative work yet.

'Moorhouse has the meanest eye and car for the cultural cliché since Mark Twain'
DON ANDERSON, THE NATIONAL TIMES

'He makes you laugh, and think'
ANGELA CARTER, THE NEW YORK TIMES